Thematic Concordance to the
Diary of St. Maria Faustina Kowalska

Compiled by
Rev. George W. Kosicki, CSB

MARIAN PRESS
STOCKBRIDGE MA 01263

2015

Available from: Marian Helpers Center, Stockbridge, MA 01263

- Prayer Line: 1-800-804-3823
- Orderline: 1-800-462-7426
- Website: www.marian.org

Library of Congress Catalog Card Number 2005929281

ISBN 978-1-59614-137-7

Front cover: Passport photo of St. Maria Faustina Kowalska and insert of the *Diary of St. Maria Faustina Kowalska*.

Formerly entitled *Study Guide to the Diary of St. Maria Faustina Kowalska*.

Printed in the United States of America

TABLE OF CONTENTS

Introduction 5

Angel(s) 8

Baptism in His Mercy 8

Bilocation 9

Cenacle 9

Chaplet 9

Church 10

Confession 10

(see Sacrament of Reconciliation)

Confessor 10

Conversations 11

Dark Night of The
Soul/Abandonment 11

Death 11

Deeds of Mercy 12

Desires/Demands of Our Lord 13

Desires of Sister Faustina 13

Dialogues (see Prayer/
Monologues)

Divine Mercy (see Mercy, Trust)

Divinization (see Transformation)

Dying 15

Eucharist 15

Father Andrasz 22

Father Bukowski 23

Father Dabrowski 23

Father Sopocko 23

Feast of Mercy 24

Fire/Flames of Love 25

Gaze 25

Gems of Sister Faustina 25

Glorifying Mercy/Glory (of) .. 29

God's Will 30

Graces 32

Health/Illness 32

Heart (of Sister Faustina) 32

Holy Spirit 33

Holy Trinity 34

Hour of Great Mercy 34

Humility 35

Hymns/Poems (of) 36

Image of The Divine Mercy .. 37

Intercession / Intercessory
Prayer 39

Judgment and Urgency. 40

Knowledge/Discernment (of) .. 40

Life of Sister Faustina 42

Love 42

Mary, Mother of God 44

Merciful Heart of Jesus 47

Mercy 50

Misery/Mercy 55

Mission of Sister Faustina 56

Mother 56

Mother Superior/General 56

New Congregation 57

Novena (for) 59

Obedience 59

Oblation/Holocaust 60

Passion 60

Peace 61

Penance   (see Sacrament of
            Reconciliation)

Places 61

Poland 61

Prayers (for) (to) (of) 62

Prayer/Monologues 66

Preaching of God's Mercy ... 68

Presence of God 68

Priests 69

Promises 69

Promotion (see Work of Mercy)

Purgatory (see Souls in
   Purgatory)

Radio 70

Rays 70

Religious Life 71

Resolutions 71

Retreat(s) 72

Sacrament of Reconciliation . 73

Introduction

The *Diary of Saint Maria Faustina Kowalska* is a personal journal which Sr. Faustina kept in response to specific instructions from God and from her spiritual director, Fr. Sopocko.

Written over a four-year period (1934-1938), the *Diary* was not intended as a systematic and organized collection of teachings, but rather as a record of Sr. Faustina's day-to-day thoughts, prayers, and experiences of the Lord. In complete obedience to the Lord's command, she simply wrote down everything He made known to her about His mercy in order to encourage people to trust in Him.

Those who have studied the *Diary* have discovered that it contains a great treasury of revelations, teachings, insights, and prayers. In addition to the many significant revelations of our Lord about trust and mercy, there are major teachings on several subjects, including the Eucharist, Confession, Mary, the spiritual life, and suffering for others. But, since the bits and pieces of these teachings are scattered throughout the more than 600 pages of the original handwritten text, some ordering and organization seems needed to make the richness of this treasury available to the reader.

The Compiler

The late Fr. George Kosicki, CSB, nurtured by a lifetime devotion to The Divine Mercy undertook a study of the *Diary*. As director of the Department of Divine Mercy at the Congregation of Marians in Stockbridge, Massachusetts, from 1986-1988, Fr. Kosicki was engaged in a full-time apostolate of writing, preaching, and directing publications on the mercy of God. His roots with the Marians go quite deep. In the 1940s his family was introduced to the Marians — and the Divine Mercy devotion — through one of the Marian publications, *Roze Z Ogrodu Maryi* (Roses from the Garden of Mary).

When Fr. George entered the novitiate of the Basilian Fathers in 1946, his mother gave him a picture of the image of the Merciful Savior, which she had received from the Marians. It hung in his room the rest of his life, a daily reminder for him to trust in the mercy of God, and a continuous spiritual connection with the Marians. After ordination in 1954, Fr. Kosicki taught and did research in biochemistry for 16 years. He spent the next 16 years writing religious articles and books and conducting renewal retreats for priests. Then, under the tutelage of Fr. Seraphim Michalenko, MIC, vice-postulator for North America for the cause of Sr. Faustina's beatification, Fr. Kosicki was prepared for his work on Divine Mercy and the *Diary*. In 1986 Father Seraphim, who had been working in Rome, decided to remain there to promote the cause of Sr. Faustina, and Fr. Kosicki was appointed to succeed him as director to the Department of Divine Mercy.

Father Kosicki then served as assistant director of Divine Mercy International, a former apostolate of the Marians of the Immaculate Conception in Stockbridge, Massachusetts. Divine Mercy International responded to the increased awareness and interest in Sr. Faustina and in the Divine Mercy message and devotion as a result of her beatification April 18, 1993.

His first tasks as director included several major projects. He coordinated the promotion of the film *Divine Mercy — No Escape* and the publication of the long-awaited English translation of the *Diary of St. Faustina*. Then came *The Promise*, the story of the film; *Mercy My Mission: The Life of Sister Faustina*; and *Now is the Time for Mercy*, which appeared in serialized form in the *Marian Helpers Bulletin*. He also produced *Come to My Mercy*, a thirteen-week talk show series for EWTN-TV.

In the course of several years of studying the *Diary of St. Faustina*, both in the original Polish and in English translation, Fr. Kosicki became more and more challenged by the need to organize the *Diary* entries so that the wealth of information it contains on various subjects could be made more readily accessible to the reader.

A great deal of work in organizing the *Diary* entries had been done by Sr. Sophia Michalenko, CMGT, in her biography of Sr. Faustina, *The Life of Faustina Kowalska* But hers was a chronological ordering of the *Diary*. She had selected the main passages that revealed the life and mission of Sr. Faustina and then rearranged them in proper time sequence, linking them together with commentaries and related historical events drawn from Sr. Faustina's letters and the testimonies of those who knew her.

Both the Polish and English editions of the *Diary* contain thematic indexes which Fr. Kosicki found useful, but they, too, were incomplete, and the more he studied the *Diary* itself, the more evident this became.

The clincher for him was when he checked for references to Our Lady. The Polish index listed only 5. The English index was a bit higher with 38

entries, but Fr. Kosicki's own study yielded 150.

A look at some other important topics revealed a similar disparity. The English index listed only 10 references to the Eucharist, the Polish only 30, but Fr. Kosicki's own research turned up over 300. There were no references to suffering in the English index. The Polish index listed 100, and Fr. Kosicki located 320.

A Thematic Concordance

Convinced of the need for a comprehensive thematic index or concordance, Fr. Kosicki resumed his own study of the *Diary* with renewed vigor. On his third reading of the *Diary* he began marking the margins of the text with code letters indicating the various topics contained in each paragraph. He continued these notations in his fourth and fifth readings, using as many as six index cards for each paragraph to indicate the various topics dealt with. Certain topics kept reoccurring, so he used them as main subject headings and sorted all the other cards under these headings.

The result was the first draft of an alphabetized index containing over 3,000 entries under 38 general headings. It was a summary of each of the *Diary's* 1,828 paragraphs according to the main topics covered and thus was an invaluable research tool for information on each topic.

After using the Index himself and conferring with colleagues to whom he had given copies of it, Fr. Kosicki concluded that, as helpful as the Index was, it was not yet detailed enough to satisfy those studying and writing about the *Diary*.

So he undertook a sixth and seventh systematic reading of the *Diary*,

breaking down each entry into more detailed topics. As he had done in his initial readings, he noted each of the new topics on index cards, along with a brief summary statement.

It was a three-year process that left him with a four-foot-long box of new index cards. He sorted the cards under topics and subtopics and then incorporated all the new information they contained into the first draft of the *Concordance*. The final result is a comprehensive index containing 96 topics and more than 7000 subtopics, many with multiple references and cross references as well.

The *Thematic Concordance* brings out not only the essential elements of the message and devotion to Divine Mercy (trust, works of mercy, Image, Feast, Chaplet, preaching, and Novena) but also the special features of Sr. Faustina's life: the Eucharist, the Sacrament of Reconciliation, Mary, the Holy Trinity, the Cross, and suffering, her religious and spiritual life of obedience and humility, and her prayers. It shows clearly that Sr. Faustina's *Diary* is a teaching on the fundamentals of the spiritual life of a Christian as well as a vehicle for spreading the message of mercy.

How to Use the Thematic Concordance

The Concordance can be used in a number of ways. Each heading, for example, has a list of entries that can be read as meditations and teachings. (The entries concerning the Eucharist provide enough material for a full retreat!)

For students and scholars, the entries are starting points for research into the nature of mercy and the many related topics. And for people interested in deepening their understanding, the *Concordance* serves as a ready key to the actual text of the revelations of our Lord to Sr. Faustina as she recorded them in her *Diary*.

The user is encouraged to review the topics that are indexed (see the Table of Contents) and to make use of the cross references, remembering that this book is not a concordance of every word, but rather a summary of each paragraph of the *Diary*, arranged by themes.

THEMATIC CONCORDANCE

to the *Diary of St. Maria Faustina Kowalska*

The numbers following the entries refer to the paragraph numbers used in both the Polish and English editions of the *Diary*.

Angel(s)

(also see **Words of Angels**)

Asked for prayers for dying, 820

Brought Communion for thirteen days, 1676

Can not approach with a storm because of the Chaplet, 1791

Can not hear confession, 1677

Cherub guards the gate, 1271

Could envy us for Communion and suffering, 1804

Creation of, 1741

Cry Holy, Holy, Holy, 1805

Defending a dying man, 1565

During the Angelus, an understanding of God's love, 1172

Giving glory, 1604

Guardian, 683

Guardian, asks for prayers for dying, 314

Guardian, help against demons, 419

Guardian, prayer to, 412

Guardian, to purgatory, 20

Guards at the Throne, 781

Guards with presence, 490

Heard at vow time, 1111

Helpless because of Chaplet, 474

Jesus, a brother not to Angel but man, 1584

Led to hell, 741

Love makes stronger than, 1632

Meditating on their sin, 1332

Mercy not comprehended by, 1553

Not united with, but man, 1231

Present to Sister Faustina, 471

Radiant spirits guarding chuches, 630

Sang out her life, 1202

Seraph surrounded by light, 1676

Sister Faustina more pleasing than, 1489

Speaks, 470

St. Michael appears to care for Sister Faustina, 706

St. Michael fulfilled God's will, 667

Tells of prayer needs, 828

To sing of mercy, 761

Worship in heaven, 779

Would not exchange places with, 1049

Baptism in His Mercy

All misery buried in mercy, 1777

Desire to be immersed, 807

Dissolving in God, 983

Drown sufferings in Merciful Heart of Jesus, 1550

Drowned in God (The Divine Mercy), 1681

Drowned in Him, 729

Drowned in love, 1676

Drowned self in His mercy, 1801

Drowning in the Lord, 1500

Embraced by mercy when saying Chaplet, 754

Happy the soul immersed in the Fountain of Mercy, 1075

Hidden in God's mercy, 751

Hiding in the depths of mercy, 791

Immerse all sinners, 206

Immerse self in mercy, 136, 815, 1361, 1553, 1572

Immerse souls: Novena to Divine Mercy, 1209, 1210, 1212, 1214, 1216, 1218, 1220, 1224, 1226, 1228

Immersed in, 137, 142, 1538

Immersed in a sea of, 694

Immersed in God, 221

Immersed in incomprehensible love and torture, 1056

Immersed in love, 890

Immersed in the Holy Trinity, 1670

In Confession, 1602

Penetrate and divinize me, 1242

Plunge all Poland into His mercy, 1188

Plunge self into mercy, 1188

Plunged into God, 708

Plunged into ocean of divinity, 969

Plunging into mercy out of desolation, 1108

Steeped in God at Communion, 1814

Thoroughly enwrapped in God, 1828

You will be imbued with my mercy, 167

Bilocation

Attending Mass, 447

Chaplet for dying man, 1797

In presence of a dying person, 1536

Cenacle

Sacrifice consummated, 684

Vision of, 684, 765

Vision of radiant Jesus, 684

Chaplet

Against God's anger, 474, 1036

Against a storm, 1731

All will be granted by, 1541

Asking according to God's will, 1731

Assistance to the dying, 810, 811, 834, 835, 1035, 1565, 1798

Booklet printed, 1379

Brings mankind closer to Jesus, 929

Community to say it, 752

Conversion and, 687

Echo of, in prayer, 648, 1604

Everything obtainable by, 1128, 1541, 1731

Father Sopocko asks for the text, 711

For a dying man, 1797

For dying, 810, 834, 835, 1035

Formula for, 476

Full text of, 476

Great graces promised, 848

Help for the dying, 834, 835

Holy God, 1604

Jesus: say for dying man, 1797

Mercy and, 848

Mercy at hour of death, 687

Mercy for sinners, 687

Mitigates God's anger, 474, 1036

Novena before Feast of Mercy, 796, 1059

Novena of 796, 851

Novena to obtain mercy for Poland, 714

Origin of, 474

Pleases Jesus, 929

Power against a storm, 1791

Prayed for rain, 1128

Prayed for three hours to relieve heat, 1128

Praying for approval of, 851
Priests to recommend, 687
Promises of the Lord for saying, 687, 754, 811, 1128, 1541
Requested by the sisters, 752
Said with arms outstretched, 934
Say, for dying sinner, 1565
Say, unceasingly, 687
Saying of, defends dying, 1541
Storm ceases, 1731
Text of, 475
With outstretched arms, 934
Words of offering, 1777

Church

As mother, 197
Deposit all daily virtues in, 1505
Graces from, on feasts, 481
Live for entire, 1505
Mission in, of Sister Faustina, 482
My mother, 1469
Sanctity useful to, 1364
Symbolized in disrepair of convent, 559
Symbolized by the Image in an enormous temple, 560
Useful to, by sanctity, 1475, 1505
Voice of God's will, 497
What a joy, 481

Confession

(see **Sacrament of Reconciliation**)

Confessor

(see also **Father Andrasz,** and **Father Sopocko, Priests, Sacrament of Reconciliation, Spiritual Director.**)
Advice of Father Andrasz on the work of mercy, 1618
Advice on begging for mercy, 1432
Advice on New Congregation as an illusion, 643
Advice to abandonment to God's will, 1206
Angels cannot hear Confession, 1677
Be faithful to God's inspirations, 637
Blame for imprudence, 937
Causes suffering when fearful, 653
Christ teaches through, 145
Complete openness with, 269
Confession to Jesus, 817
Confessors, 269, 933, 975, 1448, 1602, 1725
Direction given to Father Bukowski, 645
Father Bukowski affirms Sister Faustina, 646
Father Sopocko seen in vision, 563
Father Sopocko's visit on the works of mercy, 1252, 1260
First Confession to Father Sopocko, 263
Frankness with Confessor, 1499, 1470, 639
God acts through, 333
God's love for Fathers Andrasz and Sopocko, 676
Importance of his words, 680
Intimacy of Jesus, 1240
Jesus speaking through the priest, 637, 639, 763
Jesus speaks through the spiritual director, 967, 968
Life with the Blessed Virgin Mary, 637
Mercy is the greatest work, 637
Miracle of mercy, 1448
Need to pray for, 938
Not all are spiritual fathers, 132
Novena for, 269
Obedience to, 353, 639

Obedience to admonition, 643
On New Congregation: "Wait,"
1117
One understands, 133
Openness toward, 645
Pray for the confessor, 647
Pray much for, 647
Promise of Father Sopocko, 258
Promised on retreat, 215
Reflect on spiritual childhood,
333
Role of spiritual director, 937-
941
Sermon on mercy, 417
Speak only to, about spiritual
life, 671
Spiritual directors, 12, 362, 979,
1308, 1784
Suffering opposition, 90
Surge of light, 1617
Tell him Jesus works with weak-
ness, 498
Thanks for Father Andrasz, 1596
Thanks for Father Sopocko,
1586
Transgression against, touch
Christ, 145
Tribunal of mercy, 975, 1448
Uncertainty of, felt by Sister
Faustina, 75
Visit of Father Sopocko, 1238
Warns of illusions, 74
Welcoming home Father
Andrasz, 1168
Words of Archbishop, 473, 479
Words of Jesus about Confession
as a fountain of mercy, 1602
Words of Jesus addressed to
priests, 50, 177, 570, 687,
1521
Words of Mary addressed to
priests, 330, 1585
Words of Sister Faustina about
Fr. Andrasz and Fr. Sopocko,
86, 90, 141, 144, 145, 215,
263, 293, 330, 436, 442, 466,
494, 659, 675, 676, 677, 712,
749, 817, 879, 967, 968,
1012, 1238, 1256, 1346,
1388, 1390, 1401, 1408,
1472, 1544, 1547
Words of Sister Faustina about
priests, 302, 446, 491, 578,
806, 838, 931, 1052, 1240,
1384, 1455, 1534, 1719
Words of Sister Faustina
addressed to confessors, 34,
35, 75, 95, 99, 108, 112, 121,
122, 132, 139, 595, 721, 937-
941
Words of warning, 646

Conversations
(see also **Prayer/Monologues**)
Of the Merciful Lord, 1485,
1489
With a despairing soul, 1486
With a perfect soul, 1489
With a sinful soul, 1485
With a soul striving for perfec-
tion, 1488
With a suffering soul, 1487

Dark Night of The Soul/ Abandonment
By God, 496
Dark night of the soul, 23, 24,
78
Experience of, 109
Trial of trials, 98

Death (see also **Dying**)
Count only on mercy, 1553
Defended at, by Chaplet, 1541
Desire to die at the Lord's tim-
ing, 1539
Hymn of, 1435
Knowledge of, 1449, 1477
Last Sacraments, sudden sick-
ness, 323

Letters of sisters before, 1673
Meditation on, 1551
Preparation for, 1342
Promise of Mercy at, 48, 379, 723, 754, 811, 1075, 1520, 1540
Promotors of mercy will be shielded at, 1540
Ready for, 1679

Deeds of Mercy

Acts of mercy of spirit, 1316, 1317
Admonition, 919
Always be merciful, especially to sinners, 1446
As porter, 1267
Assisting her younger sister, 982
Aware of others praying, 1018
Be merciful, 1446, 1486, 1695
Be merciful to others, 1486
Beggar boy, 1312
Beggars treated kindly, 1282
Begging for God's pardon, 987
Carrying others' burdens, 1039
Chaplet for the dying, 1035
Comforting men out of work, 1377
Comforting the sorrowful, 1063
Consoling a troubled girl, 864
Consoling others, 871
Consoling the sorrowful, 1031
Dealing with beggars, 1282
Evidence of greatness, 663
Faustina and, 280, 1313, 1694, 1695
Feeding Jesus under the guise of the beggar boy, 1312
Feeding the poor, 1297
Five men at gate, 1377
Flow from love, 703
Flowers for a friend, 71
Forestall judgment, 1317

Forgiveness, asked by sister who made life difficult, 632
Gentleness, 1282, 1297, 1377
Gift of ears of grain, 1713
Gift of knowledge, 1283
Image reminder of the need of, 742
Kitchen work, potato draining, 65
Lord's desire for, 1249
Ministry to the dying, 935, 936
Need of, 1317
Opportunities for, 1313
Opportunity to practice toward the sick, 1269
Oranges from a sister, 1647
Patience in visits, 920
Prayer for help to perform, 163, 1242
Reflect the Lord, 1446, 1688, 1695, 1696
Reflection by Sister Faustina, 1269
Regulated by mercy, 703
Roses in potato pot, 65
Sacrifice, a mercy in spirit, 1316
Sanatorium room prepared beautifully, 1675
Service to the sick, 1029
Spiritual mercy, 1317
Strength and courage to act, 1090
Tea to a sick sister, 756
Three degrees, 163, 742
Two hungry children, 1297
Visit of a sister, 816, 864
Visit to sister with tea, 756
Ways to carry out, 742, 1156, 1157, 1158, 1316, 1317
Words of Jesus on opportunity for deeds of mercy, 1267
Words of Jesus reflecting His Merciful Heart, 1688

Desires/Demands of Our Lord

Believe my wounds, 379

Boundless trust for those seeking perfection, 1578

Chaplet, as Novena before the Feast, 796

Chaplet encouraged, 1035, 1541

Desires transformation, 726

Feast a plenary indulgence, 1109

Feast of Mercy, 49, 50, 299, 699, 965

For deeds of love, 1249

For souls like Sister Faustina, 718

For perfection of souls, 1601

Image blessed, 49, 341

Image publicly honored, 414

Mercy spread over the world, 1777

Mercy to be poured out on all, 1074

Mercy venerated, 998

None to escape mercy, 1728

Pour out mercy, 1190

Prayer for sinners, 1397

Proclaim mercy, 301

Salvation of sinners, 186

Salvation of souls, 1784

Sanctify souls, 1784

Tell the world of My mercy, 1074, 1142, 1190, 1448

That all know Him as King of Mercy, 378

Three o'clock, immerse self in mercy, 1572

To consecrate in the upper room, 832

To heal suffering mankind, 1588

To prolong the time of mercy, 1160

Tribunal of mercy, to seek comfort, 1448

Trust from creatures, 1059

Trust in mercy, graces, 687

Worship of mercy, 742

Desires of Sister Faustina (for) (to)

(See also **Saint/Sanctity: Desire to be, Souls: Desire for, Union: With God**)

Adore mercy and encourage souls to trust, 1234

All for God, 1365

All souls escape hell today, 873

An extraordinary yearning for God, 807

Be a child of the Father, 242

Be eternally united with God, 1303

Be hidden, 306

Be a host, 641

Be a living host, 908

Be a living host sacrifice, 1826

Be a priest, 302

Be a Saint (see also **Saint/Sanctity: Desire to be**), 1326, 1333, 1372, 1571

Be transformed into a hymn of glory, 1708

Be transformed into Jesus, 193

Be transformed into love, 1820

Be united to Jesus for ever, 1700

Clarify demands of Jesus, 744

Coming of the Lord, 793, 1589

Communion, 1815

Conceal suffering, 57

Day of eternity, 1230

Death, 1573

Death and eternity, 899

Desire God, 180, 672, 703, 885, 970, 1573, 1713

Die according to God's will, 1539

Do God's will always, 1729

Drinking the cup of bitterness, 1484

Dying of longing, 471, 843

Ears of grain, 1713

Eucharist when sick, 876

Every Communion, 1804

Feast, 505, 1041

Fulfill God's will, 492, 615

Glorify God's mercy, 745, 835, 836

Glorify God's will, 743

Glorify mercy in life and death and in eternity, 697, 1242

Glorify the Lord, 305

God, 180, 672, 703, 885, 970, 1573, 1713

God alone, 856, 1145, 1359

God's will, 795, 1359

God's will, souls, mercy adored, Feast, sanctity, blessing on family, priest, community, 1581

Great longing for the Lord, 413, 1710

Grows with knowledge of God, 591

Hide in Merciful Heart of Jesus, 1021

Hymn of, 1304, 1591, 1632, 1653

Intense yearning, 26

Jesus alone, 881

Keep eyes on Jesus, 1333

Know God more, 974

Last day, 825

Lead souls to mercy, 1488

Longing for God, 850, 866, 946, 1050, 1054

Longing for the Lord and death, 841

Longing of the heart, 1239

Lord, 69, 853, 867, 1137

Lord, like a soul in purgatory, 1186

Love God, 525

Love grows, 605

Love in return, 1631

Love Jesus in a special way like a fragrant rose bud, 1822

Love like no other soul, 1771

Make Jesus welcome in my heart, 1721

Make life an act of thanksgiving, 1285

Make reparation for various sins, 1248

Merciful Heart, 969

Not for a new world, but for Jesus, 587

Of God for us, 244

Of the Heart of the Lord, 1026

On seeing the stars and moon, 470

Only Jesus satisfies, 1600

Painful longing, 1100

Receive Jesus with greater fervor, 1473

Reflect His Compassion, 1242

Remove the veil of heaven, 483

Save sinners 72, 648 (see also **Sinners**)

Save souls 679, 1645 (see also **Souls**)

See God, 808

Sensing His Presence, 469

Shine with God's mercy, 617

Souls, 235, 483, 745 (see also **Souls**)

Souls to glorify mercy, 1489

Souls to trust in Mercy, 1489

Spread Divine Mercy, 745

Suffer, 507, 761, 853 (see also **Suffering**)

Suffer like Christ, 1418

Thanksgiving, 1367, 1368

That mercy be glorified, 1691

That souls praise God's mercy, 598

That souls recognize the Lord, 305

Transform me, 1289

Union with God, 761, 918, 952

Unite with desires of Jesus, 1581

What are they? 1489

World to be transformed into love, 1771

Worship be given to mercy, 1048

Yearning for God, 1121

Divine Mercy
(see **Mercy, Trust**)

Dying
(see also **Chaplet, Death, Iintercession, Souls, Souls in Purgatory**)

Chaplet for, 1035

Dying, yet not, 1054

Holy water, 601

Prayer for, 207, 687, 810, 811, 820, 835, 924, 935, 936, 971, 985, 1015, 1536, 1541, 1639, 1684, 1698, 1762, 1777, 1797

Soul, suffering Passion for, 1724

Eucharist
Accompanying Communion for the sick, 183

Act of union with all Masses in the world, 1783

Address of Pius XI to Eucharistic Congress, 925

Adoration, 319, 324, 332, 346, 355, 405, 699, 754, 865, 1443, 1692

Adoration, a consolation to Jesus, 1664

Adoration for friends, 1438

Adoration in spirit, 1025

Adoration in thanksgiving for illness, 1062

Adoration with pain because of ingratitude, 384

Agreement with doctor to receive, 878

All free time before, 1404

All good due to Holy Communion, 1392

All strength from Holy Communion, 814, 1037, 1386, 1404, 1826

Angels would envy Holy Communion and suffering, 1804

Asked for special strength to receive, 876

Assurance of victory, 91

At adoration Jesus speaks of voluntary offenses, 1641

At times the senses rejoice in, 1473

Awesome mystery of the Mass, 914

Barely managed to assist, 1089

Blessed Virgin Mary instructs during, 840

Blessing the people, 420

Blood of Jesus circulating in veins, 992

Breaking spiritual wafer, 1438

Caught up into embrace of God, 439

Cenacle, 684, 757

Cleansing by Holy Communion, 1611

Closeness with the Lord, 40, 160, 177, 493

Coming of bridegroom, 1805

Communion experience of Christ's Heart beating, 1821

Communion from an angel, 1676

Communion ... in communion with the Trinity, 451, 472, 673, 674, 1129, 1670, 1781

Communion in the hand, 160

Communion of reparation for sins of Mardi Gras, 927

Communion, prayed for healing, 1089

Condition for receiving mercy and forgiveness, 699, 1108

Conditions for receiving when sick, 878

Consecrated like Eucharist, 1564

Constant miracle of mercy, 1584

Corpus Christi procession, 1136

Darkness on not receiving, 715

Deep union, 1334

Desire for sick and suffering, 876

Desire for souls, 1249

Desire for the Lord at Communion, 1473, 1721

Desire of Jesus to unite with souls, 1385

Desire to be a Sacrificial Host, 483

Desire to be Eucharist, 641, 832

Desire to become a Host, 641

Desire to make a Holy Hour but hindered, 1276

Desire to receive with greater fervor, 1473

Discernment of ineffective priest, 1719

Divine Blood in her heart, 478

Divine Presence, 745, 969

Divinizing power, 1289

Drawing strength from, 1431

Drawn into center of love, 1121

Draws strength from the tabernacle, 1037

Drowned in love at Communion, 802

Ecstasy when contemplated, 1489

Enclosed self in tabernacle, 703

Enkindle a longing, 867

Envy of angels, 1804

Experience of God's love, 1121

Experience of grace, 1337

Experience of the Passion 384, 872, 942 (see also **Passion, Stigmata, Suffering**)

Experience of thorn, 1425

Experience of wounds of Redeemer, 942

Feast of Corpus Christi, too sick to attend Mass, 1786

Fever drops and so receives, 878

Filled with love at Communion, 493

Fire of God's love, 745

Flame from her pierced heart, 1140

For adoration, 1565

For friends, 1438

Fountain of mercy, 1487, 1817

Four hours of adoration, 355

Free time before, 82

Gaze of faithfulness, 1239

Gift of knowledge regarding a sister, 756

Glorify mercy, 1707

Greatest of all gifts, 1670

Greatest secret: Jesus in the, 1489

Healing of the tongue, 92, 590

Heart of Jesus, 223, 908, 1572, 1607

Holy Communion, 64, 206, 324, 451, 473, 556, 558, 717, 718, 1034, 1089, 1132, 1251, 1289, 1437, 1453, 1667, 1670, 1802, 1803, 1992

Holy Communion, accompanying the sick, 183

Holy Communion alone sustains, 1037

Holy Communion brought after night of suffering, 1458

Holy Communion, most precious moments, 840

Holy Communion sustains Sister Faustina, 1037

Holy fire, 1392 (see also **Fire/Flames of Love**)

Holy Hour, 85, 412, 685, 691, 1041, 1062, 1685

Holy Hour extended to three hours, 268

Holy Hour for sinners, 319

Holy Hour meditation on Incarnation, 332

Holy Hour to hasten the Feast, 1041

Holy Thursday 1938 attended, 1663

Host in the hand of Jesus, 1622

Host, my name is, 485

Host radiates, 1462

Hour of adoration in thanks for graces and illness, 1062

Humbled to dwell as bread, 1575

Hymn, 4, 159, 356, 1002, 1233, 1324, 1393, 1427, 1569, 1591, 1629 (see also **Hymns**)

Hymn of a hidden God, 1591

Infrequent reception, 1447

Instructed by Blessed Virgin Mary to prepare for, 1114

Interceding, 526, 621, 1501

Interceding for a knowledge of mercy, 1077   mercy, 1077

Interceding for a priest, 258, 1607

Interceding in union with Eucharist, 1501

Intimate union with Redeemer in Communion, 735

Invitation to dwell in the heart, 1806

Jesus always present, 575

Jesus asks for fewer words, 739

Jesus assures Sister Faustina of mercy for many souls by suffering, 1459

Jesus comes with graces—but not recognized, 1385

Jesus complains of ingratitude, 1537

Jesus enters some hearts with pain, 1598

Jesus enters some souls unwillingly, 1658

Jesus: Give me souls, 1690 Jesus hidden under Host, 1564

Jesus, Host sustains, 1620

Jesus, Host with her, 877

Jesus: I dwell in tabernacle as King of Mercy, 367

Jesus pained at, received without faith, 1288

Jesus promises protection for those who proclaim mercy, 379

Jesus suffering in some communicants, 1598

Jesus: "They are the delight of My Heart," 1176

Joy of Mass, 411

Keep watch, 854

Knowledge of Blessed Virgin Mary's concern for Jesus, 1437

Knowledge of God's holiness, 1801

Knowledge of His holiness and majesty and our misery, 1801

Knowledge of Merciful Heart of Jesus, 1142

Knowledge of work of mercy, 1143

Last Communion during a retreat, 1343

Leaves end of, 1443

Light on the New Congregation, 1154

Light received during adoration, 147

Litany, 356, 949

Living sacrifice, 908

Lord's aversion toward a certain soul, 1280

Love calls for reciprocity, 1770

Love of God at seven years, 1404

Love of the Eucharist since age seven, 1404

Love without effort of words, 739

Mary and, 840, 843, 677, 1300, 1437

Mass, 12, 21, 39, 182, 239, 345, 364, 365, 528, 615, 649, 668, 1028, 1077, 1186, 1187, 1300, 1441, 1443, 1657, 1668, 1670

Mass (experience during)
    knowledge about Father Sopocko, 1346, 1408, 1472
    knowledge of a weak priest, 1719
    presence of God's love, 870, 1129
    union with Mary, 843
    Masses offered for Father Andrasz, 1623

Meaning/reflection, 409, 914, 992, 1037, 1302, 1392, 1489

Meditation after Mass on love, 1705

Merciful Heart in Host, 223, 908, 1572 (see also **Merciful Heart of Jesus**)

Mercy, Easter procession, 1668, 1669

Mercy hidden in, 1485

Midnight Mass, vision of nativity, 1442

Miracle of mercy, 1489

Missing Mass because of sickness, 894, 1433, 1786

Most solemn moment of life, 1804

Mother Superior's powerful prayers, 1421

Mystery of Mass, 914

Name of Sister Faustina, 3

New Year's Eve of three hours adoration, 355

Not receiving because of a doubt, 156

Novena of adoration for the Feast, 1041

Novena of Communions for Poland, 1251

Offering her misery, 1803

Omitting Communion, 23, 91, 105, 156, 612

On Feast, 699

On Holy Thursday Jesus had Sister Faustina in mind, 1774

Opened wide Your mercy, 1747

Pain on not receiving Communion, 612

Patron of the year, 360

Permission to visit when sick, 1678

Power in the Host, 616

Prayer at Communion for knowledge, 1527

Prayer for healing, 1089

Prayer for silence in suffering, 896

Prayer for strength in suffering, 1484

Prayer in suffering, 1484

Prayer in union with all the Masses, 1783

Prayer of commending all needs, 1751

Prayer of transformation, 832

Prayer of trust, 25

Prayer of welcome, 1731

Prayer to be a living Host, 908

Prayer to be consecrated, 1564

Prayer to the Heart of Jesus, 1607

Prayer to the Host, 1350, 1747 (see also **Hymns, Prayers**)

Praying before the Eucharist, 278, 637, 867, 1138, 1337, 1425, 1484, 1620, 1769

Praying for the sick, 826

Praying to the Heart of Jesus, 1348

Preparation for Holy Communion, 1457, 1804, 1828

    all night, 717

    (as) for a wedding feast, 1827

    approaching mercy in misery, 1817

    the Bridegroom, 1805, 1806

    by faith, 1814

    by longing, 1813

    by showing a special love like a rosebud, 1822

    by submission, 1812

    by union of love, 1815

    communion as a child, 1818

    communion by prayer for mercy, 1803

    desire to be transformed, 1820

    for the Holy One, 1825

    for the Savior, who rescues from temptations, 1823

    God of Majesty surrounding me, 1828

    inviting Him into my heart, 1808, 1809

    the King of Glory, 1810

    the Lord who can do all things, 1825

    with joy, 1824

    with love for Him, 1807

Presence/visit/adoration, 9, 12, 23, 25, 32, 44, 71, 73, 77, 147, 152, 154, 160, 164, 165, 167, 169, 178, 187, 188, 190, 195, 213, 216, 220, 223, 224, 237, 252, 268, 338, 403, 476, 979, 1025, 1556, 1603, 1604

Presence envelops, 808

Presence felt after Communion, 318

Presence in the heart, 318

Presence of Eucharist until next Communion, 318, 1302, 1821

Presence of Holy Trinity, 486

Presence piercing, 846

Preserve my soul in whiteness, 1350

Prisoner of love, 80

Procession, 1136, 1140, 1668, 1669

Prostrate before, 77

Questioning the Lord at Communion, 1608

Radiance of the sun, 991

Rays from (see also **Rays**)

    Eucharist, 344, 370, 420, 441, 657

    Host, 336, 344, 441, 657, 1462

    Image, piercing Sacred Host, 441

    the monstrance, 370

Received in sanatorium, 1678

Receiving Communion as viaticum, 1342, 1551, 1552

    from an angel, 1676

    in her cell, 1658

    when feelings are dead, 1278

    when sick, 902

Receiving in the manner of angels, 1278

Refuge, 74

Relief from suffering during adoration, 1153

Remains in Sister Faustina, 318, 1302

Renewal of vows (in 1938), 1781

Request at Communion, 590

Request of Jesus for adoration for mercy, 1070

Sacrificial offering, 309, 385, 475, 476, 483, 531, 1622

Second Host falls, 160

Secret of all sanctity, 1489

Seldom souls unite to Jesus, 1447

Sets love aflame, 1807

Sorrow to Jesus because omitted, 612

Source of all strength and light, 704

Standing before God as a host, 1564

Strength from, 91, 224, 1037, 1386, 1826

Strength in spiritual warfare, 1498

Strength in suffering, 1509, 1620

Strength in the struggle of sickness, 876, 1310

Strength in works of mercy from Communion, 1377

Suffering for priests, 823

Strength from Communion, 1386

Suffering ceased, 1153

Suffering in spirit with Jesus, 1454

Suffering, offering, 309, 385, 475, 476, 483, 531, 1622

Suffering and the wounds of Jesus, 759

Suffering during adoration, 450

Suffering during Mass, 324, 615, 1657

Suffering of Passion, 759, 808, 927, 1276 (see also **Passion, Stigmata, Suffering**)

Sustained in suffering, 1620

Symbolized by the rays of the Image, 299

Tabernacle in Novitiate, 228

Tabernacle of mercy, 1747

Tabernacle throne of mercy, 1485

Talking with Jesus, 1292

Taken up into the Trinity during Communion, 1670 (see also **Holy Trinity**)

Taste of the Passion, 872

Temptation not to receive Communion, 673, 674

Thanking, for spiritual director, 968

Thought of Holy Communion strengthens, 1310

Time of intercession, 621

Transformed by, 160

Trinity present, 451, 486

Trust in, 1138

Under obedience not to attend Mass, 894

Union during Mass, then peace, 1262

Union with Blessed Virgin Mary, 843

Union with God, 1262, 1334

Union with Jesus, 1262

Union with Trinity, 1129 (see also **Holy Trinity**)

United with the Majesty of God, 870

United with those adoring, 1419

Urge to act, but in sanatorium, 865

Value of the Eucharist, 409

Vigil before Christmas, too sick to attend, 1441

Vigil for Holy Communion, 826

Vision of (see also **Visions**)
angel, 471
cenacle, 684, 757
child Jesus, 442
ciborium with hosts living, 640
crucified Jesus, 913, 1253
dying Jesus, 976
face of Jesus, 1420
horrible cat, 873
Host, 370, 616, 991
Hosts received by converts, 709
Infant Jesus, 659, 829, 1481
Jesus, 979, 1053
Jesus and Eucharist, 167, 177, 184, 188, 344, 442, 913
Jesus and Mary, 677
Jesus and Mary and Joseph, 846
Jesus in beauty, 1374
Jesus on the Cross, 1628
Jesus suffering, 1467, 1512, 1599
living Hosts, 640, 1407
majestic Jesus, 1246
Mass in homes, light only from the Eucharist, 991
Passion during adoration, 445
Pope saying Mass, 368
rays from the host, 336, 344, 441, 657
wounds, 252
Vision of Christ, in Communion, with sinners, 1280
Vision of Jesus at adoration as in Image, 560
Vision of Jesus during Eucharist, (see also **Visions of Eucharist, Visions of Jesus**)

as in Image, 473, 500, 560, 613
as infant and Our Lady, 529, 846
at adoration suffering, 614, 669
at Benediction, 626
at Communion, 439, 498,707, 1280
at Mass, 411, 438, 1053
at Mass, crucified, 669, 913, 1032, 1253, 1512
at Mass, dying on the cross, 1512
at Mass as a child, 447, 560, 1820
at Mass as infant, 829, 1481
at Mass suffering, 1467
celebration in Rome, 1044-1048
crucified, 913, 1032
during Holy Thursday Mass, 1663
dying, 976
face, 433, 1420
His desire for union, 1385, 1669
Holy Hour, 691
in Cenacle, 684, 757
in His majesty, 1246
in Passion, 413, 913, 964, 1032, 1599, 1628
in splendor, 1067
in the monstrance during adoration, 406, 1420
infant, 406, 447, 560, 562, 575, 597, 659, 829, 847, 879, 1346, 1481, 1820
on the cross, 1628
regularly, 434
suffering, 413, 964
with rays, 473, 500, 560, 613, 1046

Visit during sickness, 801
Visit to Blessed Sacrament
   urged, 1572
Visit to churches and chapels in
   spirit, 1501
Vivid presence of God, 1611
Weakness during, 1657
Welcome Jesus into my heart,
   1721
What mysteries at Mass, 914
With pain because of ingrati
   tude, 384
Words of Jesus, during Eucharist
   about,
      delighting His Heart, 1176
      desire of Jesus for union,
      1385
      desire of Jesus to come,
      451, 1458, 1459
      Eucharist, 1385, 1407,
      1447, 1485, 1683, 1770,
      1811, 1816, 1820, 1824,
      1826
      fearing nothing, 258, 634
      giving Him souls, 1690
      His love, 1292
      humility, 1293
      indifferent souls, 1447,
      1537
      knowing the depths of His
      mercy, 873
      leaving Self in the
      Eucharist, 1774
      love as consoling, 1664
      lukewarm communicants,
      1288
      meeting Sister Faustina,
      1705
      mercy to sinners, 1665
      misery and mercy, 718
      peace, 865
      praising Him, 1707
      prayer for Russia, 818

      proclaiming mercy, 1519
      standing ready, 854
      submission, 954
      time of suffering, 1697
      voluntary offenses, 1641
      works of mercy, 1519, 1667
Your Eucharistic love sets Sister
   Faustina on fire with love for
   neighbor, 1769

Father Andrasz

(see also **Confessor,**
Spiritual Director)
Advice of, in dryness and on
   communing with Jesus, 1243
Advice on sufferings, put your-
   self in the hands of Blessed
   Virgin Mary, 1243
Advice regarding leaving con-
   gregation, 655, 658
And Fr. Sopocko writing with
   flashes of light, 675
Answers all her queries, 749
At prayer, 1529
Away, 1161, 1162
Be a child toward, 1544
Breaks up the Child Jesus, 677
Caution regarding sudden
   apparitions, 1068
Celebrates Mass, 847
Comforts Sister Faustina, 715
Confession in Pradnik, 817
Confession to, 1617
Complete confidence in, 494
Confronts Sister Faustina on
   leaving, 655
Counsel of, 55
Delay in telling him about
   Novena of Chaplets, 714
Direction before final vows, 141
Feared by Satan, 1405
Friend of the Heart of Jesus,
   967, 1163
Grace of union with God, 769

Holy Spirit is your principal spiritual director, 658

Live by faith, pray for the work of Divine Mercy, 1618

Make a novena to know God's will regarding the New Congregation, 665

Mass offered by, 659

Mass with vision of Jesus and Mary, 677

Month of Masses for, 1623

Need a group to beg mercy, 623

No dispensation from inspirations, 52

Pleasing child of God, 1388

Pleasing to God, 1012

Questions about the work of mercy postponed, 847

Replaces Jesus, 1308

Returns from Rome, 1168

Saint pleasing to God, 978

Special devotion to Blessed Virgin Mary, 1388

Spiritual counsel, 506

Surprise at Sister Faustina's actions, 1596

Talked about to the Lord, 676

Vision of Jesus, He will lead you, 712

Vision of saying Mass and infant Jesus, 879

Father Bukowski

Affirms Sister Faustina, 646

Admonition of, 643

Father Dabrowski

Advice of, 271

Prayer for, 272

Father Sopocko

Advice, 270

Advice on holy indifference, 1255

And Father Andrasz writing with flashes of light, 675

At his desk despite fatigue, 762

At Mass, vision of Christ Child and Mary, 597

At present, filled with bitterness, 1390

By letter, God is conducting the work of mercy, 764

Conversation with, 1254

Conversation with God not to be avoided, 430

Direction before final vows, 141

Discernment of his soul, 604

Draws strength from the Lord alone, 838

Feared by Satan, 1405

Giving glory by his work, 1472

Grace of union with God, 769

Hated by Satan, 1384

His heart a heaven, 574

Humble submission to, 144

Jesus: a priest after My Heart, 1256

Letter about publishing a mercy card, 711

Letter from, 667

Loved by the Lord, 63

Mass by, vision of Jesus, 1408

Opposition to, 1272

Pleasing to God, 962

Pleasing to God, yet crucified, 1253

Prayer of thanks for, 1586

Priest entirely filled with God, 1238

Promise of prayer for, 596

Receives ingratitude, 1547

Regard for God's glory only, 1384

Resembles Crucified Jesus, 1259

Saying Mass, 345

Saying Mass and vision of Child Jesus, 312

Suffering of, 86, 596, 604

Suffering because of mercy work, 422

Suffering followed by joy, 578

Suffering in solitude and humility, 838

Talked about to the Lord, 676

Thoughts united to those of Jesus, 1408

Triple crown, 596, 604

Vision of, 53, 61

Vision of working at desk with a halo, 762

Visit about work of mercy, 1252

Visit in response to prayer, 1238

Work progressing, 1401

Working to present work of mercy, 1390

Writes of poor health, 959

Writing and Absolution, 1256

Feast of Mercy

Celebrated by Sister Faustina, 280

Celebrated (in 1935), 420

Clarification by Jesus of, 341

Command to celebrate, 280

Communion and Confession, 699

Complete remission of sins and punishment on, 300

Conclusion of Jubilee Year of Redemption (in 1935), 420

Conditions for complete forgiveness on, 699, 1109

Conversation with Father Sopocko about, 1254

Deeds of mercy along with, 206, 742

Desire of Jesus for, 49, 299, 711, 998

Desire of Sister Faustina, 711, 1041

Disputes about, 1110

Emerged from tenderness, 699

Emerged from the depths of God's mercy, 420

Floodgates open, 699

From depths, for consolation, 1517

Goodness of God and, 458

Healing and strengthening needy souls on, 206

Heart of Jesus rejoices in, 998

Importance to Our Lord of, 420, 998, 1517

Inspires trust, 570

Intercession for, 1041

In union with suffering, 784

Jesus commands a Novena, 1059

Last hope of salvation, 965, 998

Neglect of, 341

Novena of Chaplets, 796

Oblation for, 206, 1680

Offered self at holocaust for sinners, 1680

Prayer for, 341 "O Blood and Water...", 1003, 1041

Prayer to hasten, 1003

Priests to proclaim mercy, 50, 570

Promise of complete remission, 1109

Promise of presence at, 1042

Refuge and shelter for all, especially poor sinners, 699

Satan: do not pray for, 1497

Sunday after Easter as the Feast of Mercy, 49, 88, 280, 299, 420, 570, 699, 742

Time to turn to mercy, 570

Union with Holy Trinity, 1073 (see also **Holy Trinity**)

Urgency of, 965

Vision of crowds, 1046

Vision of Feast celebrated in Rome, 1044

Vision of Jesus as in Image,
1048
Why? 341
Will celebrate interiorly, 711
Worship of mercy, 742

Fire/Flames of Love
Ardor in the heart to act, 569
Burning within, 491
Burns as victim of love, 726
Compassion for sinners, 1521
Desire for, 507
Enkindled her soul, 439
For souls, 745
From Host pierced her heart,
1140
Heart burning with love, 1705
Heart to burn with eternal, 1230
In her heart, 432, 459, 587
Inflamed in His love, 1828
Living flame almost consumed
by, 1776
Love, 1082, 1100
Love aflame by Communion,
1808, 1809
Love as ray striking the heart,
1462
Love burns, 760
Love in the heart, 1096
Love joined to eternal love,
1056
Love on, 1289
Love on considering God's love,
1755
Love sets heart on fire, 1050
Of Eucharist transforms, 1392
Of God's love, 490, 745, 1104
Of gratitude, 1369
Prayer for, 495
Prayer to Blessed Virgin Mary to
enkindle the heart, 1114
Pure love burns ceaselessly,
1523

Religious, 572
Supplication, 483
Transformed into, a flame of
love, 1456
Transformed into by the
Eucharist, 160

Gaze
At the vision of the Image, 47
Desire to keep eyes fixed on
Jesus, 1333
From the Image as from the
Cross, 326
Into the abyss of mercy, 206
Jesus: fix your eyes on me, 527
Jesus: my gaze is fixed on him
(Fr. Sopocko), 86
On the Merciful Heart, 177,
1663
Sense of the Lord's, 411
Upon abyss of mercy, 1345
Upon the spouse, 252

Gems of Sister Faustina
(see also **God's Will, Humility,
Silence, Suffering**)

Abandonment is a cause for
examination, 1315
All health and strength from
God, 898
All souls depend on God, 1315
All that is beautiful is a grace of
God, 1734
All things can be done with
grace, 1696
All to please God, 1493
All with and through Jesus, 250
Allow me to see contentment in
Your Face, 1562
Armed with patience to listen,
1376
Astonished that Jesus can hide
so long, 1239
At times it is best to leave all to

Jesus, 1179

At times the senses rejoice at the coming of the Lord in Communion, 1473

Baptism unites us with other souls, 391

Beautiful and real world of the spirit, 884

Before every major grace a test, 108

Christ, the best of teachers, 66

Canary at window, 907

Chosen souls keep the world in existence, 1533

Community life is difficult but even more with proud souls, 1522

Consecrate me like a host, 1564

Constant watch on silence, 1340

Constantly discovering faults in self, 900

Damnation is for those who choose it, 631

Day of graces, Tuesday of Holy Week, 1043

Deify my actions, 1371

Despite peace, a battle to stay faithful, 1173

Divine light can work in a moment, 1250

Do all to please God and only God, 1549

Do with me as You please, 1795

Eternity is incomprehensible, 578

Every moment is filled with prayer, suffering, and work, 1545

Fear only offending God, 571

Following Christ from crib to cross, 1580

For genuine virtue there must be sacrifice, 1358

For God to act the soul must stop acting on its own, 1790

Forgiveness prepares for graces, 390

Fountain of happiness is God in the Soul, 887

Give me a great intellect to know You better, 1474

Glorifying lifts up, 1246

God cannot be happy without me, 1120

God comes to our aid, but we must ask for it, 1495

God is my creator and goal, 1329

God loves those we love, 1438

God's anger vanishes before humble souls, 1436

God's love and mine are fused as one, 1334

God's love flows through sacrifice, 1358

God strips a soul He loves, 1259

God withholds punishments because of suffering souls, 1268

Grace from offering act of patience, 1311

Grace poorly used, 1258

Graces granted by inspiration and by enlightenment, 392

Greater the suffering the more like Jesus, 1394

Greatest power hidden in patience, 1514

Happiness is interior where God dwells, 454

Happiness of others fills my soul with a new joy, 1671

Heart exposed to God like crystals, to rays, 1336

Hide me in your wound of mercy, 1631

How good to act under inspiration, 1377

How great an influence by small actions, 1475

How little people talk about Jesus, 804

How mercifully God judges according to our conscience, 1456

Humdrum days are festive, 1373

I am a royal child, 992

I can not bear flattery, 1502

I can not bring forth the fire of love, but I gaze faithfully, 1239

I desire to be a Saint, 1326

I did not know such suffering could exist, 1558

I do not fear because I know your mercy, 1803

I do not recall any conscious and voluntary transgression of the rule or vows, 1764

I do what pleases Jesus more, 380

I drown suffering in the Merciful Heart of Jesus, 1550

I feel completely like a child of God, 1818

I know I am nothing, so humiliations will be a refreshment, 1559

I love You for Yourself alone, 1794

I only know that I love and am loved, 1828

I steep self in thanksgiving, 1367

I will put Your gifts to best use, not considering the vessel they come in, 1599

I will remember you before God's Throne, 1614

I will rise, if I live in Him, 392

If given a second life, I could not do better, 1545

If God demands a sacrifice, He gives the grace, 1341

Important to beg for grace for conversations, 1495

Important to pray for the dying, 1035

In consolation I could only utter "Jesus", 1246

In doubt, clarify with spiritual director, 1550

In fear, I nestle close to the Heart of Jesus, 1726

Insect—in the winter, 922

Jesus,

    addressed as Mother, 298

    blesses the people on the Feast, 1048

    comforted me, 1349

    Divine Madman, 278

    fulfills secret wishes, 360

    gave me a lesson of humility after terrifying suffering, 1559

    instructs during seclusion, 824

    judges by our conscience, 1456, 1470

    laid the foundations of sanctity, 1331

    looks severely at certain sisters, 383

    on the Cross, model for all actions, 1333

    rebuked me for not telling of a discernment, 1424

    sanctify and fortify me, 1490

    save me, 1558

    You suffice for all, 1655

    You surpass all Mothers, 1490

Kindness of Jesus, 205

Lesson of peace in suffering, 1467

Life flows in peaceful awareness of God, 887

Life is a constant effort to do God's will, 1740

Live in the present moment, 1400

Living in the present moment, for glory of God and souls, 1183

Locked in the Merciful Heart of Jesus, 1535

Lord gives grace for what He demands, 1090

Lord likes to be always with us, 1793

Love God because He is merciful, 1372

Love must be reciprocal, 389

Making use of the present, 351

Marveling at how much God loves us, 1292

May God's Image reflect in me, 1336

May purity of intention be pleasing to You, 1740

Mercy runs through our life like a golden thread, 1466

Misery is my possession, 1630

Monotonous day, grace of, 244, 245

More beautiful the work, the more terrible the storms, 1401

More pursued with mercy, the more justly will soul be treated, 1274

Most pleasant moments are in conversing with the Lord, 1793

My heart enjoys solitude alone with God, 1395

My heart is a living tabernacle, 1302

My soul is a hymn of mercy, 1794

Need of pure intention, 484

No greater happiness than to know I please God and He loves me, 1121

Nothing happens by accident, 1530

On the Trinity, 148

One word from a soul in union with God is precious, 1595

Only by sacrifice can a soul be useful, 1358

People do not know how to perceive the soul, 1445

Personal sanctity is useful to the Church, 1364

Power of short moments, of intense presence, remain afterwards, 411

Prayer more useful than advice in some cases, 1290

Prayer to be faithful to inspirations, 1557

Profound undisturbed peace, 1366

Protect me from spiritual blindness, 1766

Purer the soul, the greater communion with God, 1270

Questioned sisters about adoration time, 1422

Rejoice at being little, 1417

Repentance transforms the soul, 388

Resolution to be faithful to the tiniest graces, 716

Resolved to fix eyes on Jesus, 1483

Resolved to follow the Merciful Jesus, 1175

Response to grace, God alone arranges, 121

Sad because Jesus suffers, 580

Secrets known only to Jesus, 201

Sisters are angels but with

human bodies, 1126

Soul that loves God is protected, 1094

Souls closest to Jesus taste bitterness, 1402

Souls especially chosen, 1556

Souls living in love are enlightened, 1191

Souls that reject mercy choose hell, 1698

Spends all free time before Eucharist, 1404

Spiritual sharing with visiting sister, 864

Splendor of the name of Jesus, 862

Strengthened by conversation with Jesus, 610

Struggles prior to great graces, 1100

Suffering for you is the delight of my heart, 1662

Suffering, the surest way, 1394

Surprised at jealousy, 633

To accept grace we need self-denial, 392

Transform me into a living host, 1826

Treats beggars like the Lord, 1282

Trust wears a crown of thorns, 1482

We resemble God most when we forgive, 1148

What is done out of love is not small, 1310

When in doubt I ask love, 1354

When misunderstood I stay with the Lord alone, 1461

When you give us what we ask for we don't accept it, 1524

Without Jesus I can do nothing, 1294

Wonder of defense by Jesus, 600

Workers often experience the fruit only in heaven, 1402

You are unchangeable but my mood changes, 1489

Glorifying Mercy/Glory (of)

Adore My mercy (Jesus), 1578

All for, 240, 1549, 1596

All will glorify mercy, 1789

At three o'clock, 1572

Because of the Image, God is receiving, 1789

Beg for graces for all to, 1160

Both misery and strength give praise to God, 1740

By,

  begging for mercy, 1488

  faithfully fighting Satan, 1499

  fighting spiritual warfare, 1560

  glorifying God, I am lifted up, 1246

  obedience over penance, 894

  proclaiming mercy, 379

  Saints, 745

  submitting to God's will, 904, 1487

  trust, 930

  work of Father Sopocko, 1472

  work of mercy, 1463

  writing under obedience, 1567 (see also **Obedience, Writing**)

Call to adore mercy, 965

Claimed by Jesus, 1572

Could not give, if no Eucharist, 1037

Demanded by Jesus, 742

Desire for, 1691

Desire of Jesus that mercy be

glorified, 998

Desire that souls, 1489

Desire to, 835

Desire to be transformed into a hymn of, 1708

Dispels Satan, 520

Eternity hardly sufficient to, 1486

Every moment, 1545

Fight for, 1548

For beauty of the earth, 1749

For four months at Pradnik, 1066

Give all to God, 148

Given by fulfilling God's desires, 500

Great desire for, 305

Greatest, 930

Holy Trinity, 1007, 1819 (see also **Holy Trinity**)

Hymn of, 1000, 1298, 1324, 1652, 1718, 1742, 1750 (see also **Hymns**)

In heaven, 753

Inspired hymns of praise, 1593

Living for, 1183

Many souls, 1073

Mercy, 5, 163, 1005, 1007, 1485, 1692, 1707, 1708

Mercy in life and death and eternity, 697

Mercy Novena, 1224

Multitudes worshipping, 848

My mercy, immerse all sinners in, 206

My soul is a hymn of adoration of mercy, 1794

Names in the book of life, 689

On earth, 753

Purpose of life of Sister Faustina, 729, 1242

Prayer for, 727, 1325, 1584

Prayer, that all venerate His

mercy, 1048

Praise of, 1590

Praise of Incarnate Mercy, 1745

Praise of redemption, 1747

Praise of Trinity, 1064

Proclaiming mercy, 379

Resounding, 1659

See the glory of The Divine Mercy, 1681

Seeing Father Sopocko, 1238 (see also **Father Sopocko**)

So great, dare not describe, 1604

Through eternity, 1553

Through the work of Father Sopocko, 1256

Trust, 930

To God for ever, 283

Uniquely as exclusive task of life, 729, 1242

Versus self glory, 1149

Will of God, 743

With every heart beat, 1234

With heart, as in heaven, 1385

With the Heart of Jesus, 836

God's Will

Abandonment to, 134, 696, 1145, 1169, 1204

Abandonment to, in suffering, 696

Accept everything, 1053, 1549, 1625

Act of total abandonment, 1264

Adored and blessed by Sister Faustina, 678

All depends on, 1642

Always did it, 666

Always, everywhere, in everything, 374

All to please God, 1493

Always fulfilled, 1667

Asked for healing as a sign of, 1091

Awareness of, 615
Battle to follow, 1173
Be done in suffering, 1237
Constant effort to do, 1740
Continually ponder, 652
Daily food, 652
Deeper knowledge of, 1394
Delight of heart, 650
Desire for, 1359
Desire to do always, 1729
Desire to fulfill, 615
Directs a sister, 993, 1009
Do with me as You will, 1085
Doing, 603
Doing always, 1328
Doing God's will is holiness, 603
Drawing strength from Eucharist to accept, 1431
Drive away all else, 638
Essence of virtues, 678
Everything depends on it, 1409
Everything, nourishment and delight, 952
Faithful submission to, 724
Forms her heart, 1024
Foundation of sanctity, 1107
Fulfilled on earth, 897
Fulfilling as faithfully as possible, 650
Given over to, 589
Greater than fasts and penances, 724
Happiness in, 775
Hymn of, 995, 1004 (see also **Hymns**)
Illumines the soul, 1351
In accord with leaving the community, 751
In appointment to Vilnius, 251
In smallest things, 639
In suffering, 496

In the voice of the Church, 497
Jesus delights in submission, 954
Jesus, You love me because of, 707
Joining our wills to, 462
Joy in, 515
Knowledge of, in a higher way, 956
Last days, according to, 1574
Life of soul, 6
Live according to it, 443
Lives by, 678
Living according to, pleases God, 821
Lord's turn to act regarding the New Congregation, 751
Love and mercy itself, 1264
Love consists in doing, 616
Love of, 725
Makes a soul truly free, 462
Measures of happiness, 518
Mercy itself, 1552, 1574
No release from, 787
Nothing can block it [New Congregation], 665
Nothing happens without it, 1208
Nothing will happen against God's will, 541
Nourished by, in suffering, 195
Nourished on, 886
Nourishment, 667, 899
Offering to, 923
Once known, it must be done, 1101
Perfection and sanctity in doing, 666
Prayer for, 328
Prayer for doing, 688
Prayer for total abandonment to, 1265
Prayer of faithfulness to, 1570

Prayer to Divine Will, 1003
Prayer to do, faithfully, 830
Prayer to fulfill, 663
Prayers of Chaplet answered
according to, 1731
Raises soul to sanctity, 1487
Ready to accept in every detail,
1356
Ready to do, 650
Resigned to, in sickness, 795
Resolution to do, 861
Revealed through Father
Sopocko, 959
Sacrifice of self will, 957
Saint Michael fulfilled, 667
Seeking to accept, 1439
Self will acknowledged, 364
Self will cancelled out, 374
Smallest thing doesn't happen
without, 1262
Sought since youth, 1504
Source of joy, 1403
Striving to reach, 444
Strong urge to carry out God's
plan, 615
Submission to, 981, 1394, 1624
Submission to in suffering, 1656
Submitted to in final sickness,
1787
Submitting to, 624
Submitting to, gives glory to
God, 904
Submitting to, in suffering, 724,
782, 972, 1204, 1496
Superior's will, 329
Surrender of sickness to, 1648,
1679
Surrender to, 1450
Surrender to life or death, 918
Three degrees of, 444
Throne, for faithfullness to, 683
To be carried out, 493
Total dependence upon, 1625

Trinity delights in submission to,
955
Union with, 582
We need to pray to submit to,
1525
Will not change in regard to
work of mercy, 1389
Yet to be completed in Sister
Faustina, 675

Graces
After a trial, a time of graces,
121
At the end of prayer, 268
Cooperating with, 204
Draws other graces, 263
Our part is not to oppose, 283
Received with thanks, 266
To overcome difficulties, 287
Wasted, 145
Watching for, 138

Health/Illness
(see also **Suffering**)
A constant effort to measure up,
1310
Effort to carry out duties, 1314
Feel decay of a corpse, 1428
Smell of decaying by a sister,
1430
Struggle to hear, 1341
Suddenly restored, 1089
Which is more pleasing? 1125
Worse, but still up, 1554

Heart (of Sister Faustina)
(**partial listing**)
Adoring Jesus in Communion,
1821
At Communion, an invitation to
dwell in, 1806
Burning with love for God, 1755
Cell for Jesus, 16
Christ's heaven, 239
Constantly united, 1806

Conversing from, 581
Crushed, but trusting, 1552
Crushed if not reconciled, 1562
Desire for Eucharist, 876
Dissolves with joy, 1553
Drawn, a hymn, 1591
Dwelling, 723
Dwelling for God, 909
Dwelling for Jesus, 193
Dying of longing, 1026
Enlightened and inspired by Jesus, 1489
Every movement of, seen by Jesus, 1176
Feeling of God's gaze, 1391
Formed by divine wishes, 1024
Freshness of captivates Jesus, 1546
Gives glory by Eucharist in, 1037
God delights in the love of, 278
God delights in a pure, 1706
God gazes into, 1025
God's dwelling, 726, 1575
God's love in, 1030
Happy in solitude, 1395
Holy temple, 1392
Hymn of desires, 1632
In ceaseless ecstasy, 1057
Jesus close to, 1481
Jesus comes to, in Communion, 1809, 1810
Jesus concerned about every beat of, 1542
Jesus, delight of, 306, 1245
Jesus invited into, at Communion, 1808
Jesus is King of, 1811
Jesus rests in, 160, 866
Jesus reposes in, 268
Kindled by love, 162
Known only by Jesus, 201

Languishing for God, 1050
Listening to the Lord with, 584
Living tabernacle, 1302
Longing for Lord, 867, 1239
Modeled after Merciful Heart of Jesus, 167
Movements of, known by Jesus, 588
Occupied by God, 1573
Offered like a fragrant rose bud, 1822
Open to suffering of others, 871
Opened and given to Jesus, 1064
Pain pierces because of souls who spurn Mercy, 1439
Peace enters in, 1609
Pierced by flame, 1140 (see also **Fire/Flames of Love**)
Place of His rest, 581
Placed on the paten, 239
Prayer for renewed, 1344
Prayer to be transformed, 514
Prepared for the coming of the King, 1810
Presence of God in, 582
Reflect the compassion of Jesus' Heart, 1688
Reflect on His words, 584
Resting in, 162
Secrets of Sister Faustina, pardon of sin, Church, tribunal of mercy, Eucharist, 1489
Strive to bear fruit, 1364
Struck by a light from the Host, 1462
Taken away, 42
Touch of eternal love, 946
Trembles with joy and love, 1824
United to Jesus by vows, 1754
Weak, but taught by God, 1331
Welcome Jesus into, 1721

Holy Spirit
(see also **Holy Trinity**)
Direct and form my soul, 825
Entering into, 1224
Faithfulness to, 291, 1504, 1556, 1557, 1828
Following, 148
Guidance of, 1326
Holiness, 291
Holy Trinity, 472
Hymn to, 1411
In the heart, 486
In you, 346
Influence, 359
Inspirations, 359, 1557
Lack of, 1478
Led by, 293
Life of Trinity, 392 (see also **Holy Trinity**)
Light of, 1052
Novena that Holy Spirit inspire Pope regarding Feast, 1041
Novena to, 269, 1090, 1752
Peace, 589, 761
Pray to, 56, 170, 1174, 1567
Prayer for confessor, 647, 968
Prayer for prudence, 1106
Retreat before Pentecost, 1709
Rule of life, 438
Shortest route, 291
Silence, 477
Spiritual director, 658
Thanks to, 1286
To inspire priests, 1041
Touches of, 1556
Union with, 1781

Holy Trinity
Adored, 5
All Three Persons love, 392
At the throne of, 85
Contemplated in heaven, 777
Creating out of mercy, 1741
Delights in you, 955
Desire to love, 283
Desire to shine in the crown of mercy, 617
Drawn into, 1020
Dwelling within, 175
Glorified at Communion, 1819
Greatest of mercy, 361
Immersed in, 1121
In heart, 27
Inaccessible light, 30
Indwelling of, 478
Lifted up to, 734
Love of and love for, 239
One but Three Persons, 911
Plunged into, 1439
Praise of, 81, 576, 1064
Prayer to, 163, 501, 525
Presence of, 486, 911
Professing faith in terrible darkness, 1558
Reflections on, 30, 148, 1474
Streams from, 918
Thrice Holy, 36
Totally immersed in, 1056
Trust in, 357
Union with, 472, 1129
Various degrees of glory, 605
You are our dwelling place, 451

Hour of Great Mercy
Discipline time, 565
Good Friday 1936, vision of Passion, 648
Immerse self in mercy, stations of cross, 1572
Implore God's mercy, 1320
Prayer, 1319
Promises attached to, 1320, 1572
Request of Jesus
    to implore mercy especially for sinners at, 1320, 1572

to practice certain devotions
daily at, 1572

Vision of Jesus crucified at, 648,
1058

Humility

(see also **Spiritual Life**)

Accepting help, 329

Advice of Mary, 1244

Advice of retreat confessor, 174

Amazed at God's, 1523

And trust, 593

As children, 722

Asking for milder food, 1429

Aware of littleness, 1500

Aware of misery, 493

Aware that God is our strength
in weakness, 495

Be faithful to God and humble,
132

Bear suffering with, 786

Benefit from, 1566

Cannot please God without it,
270

Child-like spirit, 332

Christ teaching, 184

Coming out of tribulations, a
soul is deeply humble, 115

Confession, most humiliating,
377

Constant lot of humiliations, 746

Conversation with a despairing
soul, show even a flicker of
good will, 1486

Counsel of Father Andrasz, 55,
506

Crushed like violets, 255

Daily food, 92

Desire of Mary, humility of
those in the New
Congregation, 1244

Doubts because of misery, 464

Draws down Jesus, 512

Draws down mercy on souls, 178

Draws Jesus, 1109

Envy in religious life, 833

Exercised in, since novitiate,
1503

Flood gates of heaven are open
to, 1306

Foundation of union, 587

Give first place to others, 789

God arranges everything, 120

God cannot exalt the proud,
1170

God delights in, 1092

God descended, 1057

God guards a soul that is, 1440

God stoops to the humble, 460

Grace of visitation is not slow to
a humble heart, 1734

Great humbling of Jesus in the
cenacle, 757

Has great influence, 1475

Hidden like a tiny flower, 591

Humble self profoundly, 1361

Humble souls always profit, 132

Humble souls are strong, 450

Humble souls enjoy special
favors, 778

Humiliated by superiors, 128,
133

Humiliations and, 593

In the last place, 201

Jesus: I keep company with you
to teach you humility, 184

Jesus is strength in weakness,
602

Jesus: strive for meekness and
humility, 1486

Jesus: understand that I am meek
and humble of heart, 526

Joy in humble work, 549

Knowledge of nothingness, 702

Knowledge of self, 66

Learned from the Passion, 267

Lesson in deep, 1559

Like the Heart of Jesus, 1701

Listen patiently, 789

Lonely flower, how few possess it, 1306

Lord lifts up the humble, 282

Love of, by the New Congregation, 538

Members of the New Congregation to be, 532

More humbled, the more God is present, 1605

Most precious, so few possess it, 1436

Nothing but the truth, 1502

Nothing is difficult for the humble, 93

Of God, 182

Of God in the Eucharist, 870

Of Jesus demanded of Sister Faustina, 758

Of simple service, 508

Only happiness, 593

Pay no heed to humiliations, 1360

Pleases Jesus, 1563

Pleasing to God, 1083

Plunging into, 1661

Practice asked by Jesus, 1779

Practice of virtues of humility, purity, and love of God, 1624

Pure soul is, 576

Rejoice at being little, 1417

Rejoice in, 270

Request of Blessed Virgin Mary, 1415

Resolutions of retreat, 504

Resolution to be open with the spiritual director, 861

Response to storms, 792

Sacrifice is to be pure and, 1767

Simplicity more pleasing than mortification, 1617

Sixth day of Novena: bring to me humble souls, 1220-1223

So few are humble, so few are saints, 1306

Soul kept in, 1063

Soul penetrated by humility and love of the Mother of God, 843

Souls inundated by torrents of graces, 1602

Spiritual childhood, 335

Super abundance of grace to, 1293

Taught by Blessed Virgin Mary, 620

Teaching by Blessed Virgin Mary, 1711

Thanks for humiliations, 243

Three words of Sister Faustina to a striving soul, openness, humility and obedience, 113

Training of novices, 544

True greatness, 427

True greatness in, 424

Unrecognized intentions, 511

Hymns/Poems (of)
(see also **Prayers, Prayer Monologes**)

Adore the mercy of the Lord, 1652

Beauty of creation, praise of, 1749

Creation glorifies mercy, 1750

Day of eternity, 1230

Death, 1435

Desires of my heart, 1304, 1591, 1632

Eucharist, 4, 159, 1003, 1233, 1324, 1393, 1427, 1591, 1629

Eucharist and love, 1569

Exchange of hearts, 1718

Glorifying God for creating man, 1744

Glorifying the merciful Creator,

1742

God hidden in the Host, 1591

God's mercy our strength in weakness, 482

Heart of Jesus, 1321

Holy Spirit, 1411

Holy will of God, 1004

Host of Jesus, 1629

Humble abiding, of Jesus, 1231

Image and mercy, 2

Image of The Divine Mercy, 1

Immaculate Virgin, 161

In suffering, 1479

Inspired by God, 1593

Jesus crucified, strength in suffering, 1151

Jesus hidden in the Eucharist, 1427

Jesus in my heart, 1231

Litany of mercy, 949

Longing for God, 1230, 1304, 1653

Love and Eucharist, 1569

Love and suffering, 995

Love of God in this vale of tears, 1132

Love of the hidden God, 524

Mary, 161, 1735

Mary Immaculate, my model, 1232

Merciful Heart of Jesus, 522, 1298, 1321, 1629

Mercy, 522, 1298, 1746

Mercy and glorifying, 1750

Mercy and love, 1631

Mercy in redemption, 1748, 1749

Mercy in the Incarnation, 1746

Novena to mercy, 1209 - 1229

O Sacred Host, 1233

On being a Host, 1629

Pain, 1151

Praise for mankind, 1744

Present moment, 2

Silence on, 1718

Solitude on, 1699

Spiritual warfare, 1742

Storms of life, 1322

Suffering with Christ, 1479, 1654

Thanksgiving for graces, 1286

Trinity, 1742

Trust, 1322

Trust and Eucharist, 4

Vale of tears, 1132

Virginity, 1735

Waiting for the coming of the Lord, 1589

Worship of God, 1324

Image of The Divine Mercy

Anniversary of painting, 863

Article on, 1081

Blessing of, 49, 341

Booklet printed, 1379

Cause of ecstasy, 1299, 1300

Comes alive at preaching of Divine Mercy, 417

Confessor's advice about painting, 49

Decorating the Image, 421

Disappointment in painting of, 313

Display of, on First Sunday after Easter, 88

Displayed in 1935, hands move in blessing, 416

During Holy Hour, 560

During Mass, 500

Effect of, 1379

Exposition of, in church, 570

Fathers Andrasz and Sopocko at feet of, 675

Feast and, 742

Feast of Corpus Christi, 441

Gaze of Jesus from, 326
Glory flowing from, 1789
Grace of baptism for a Jewish
lady, 916
Graces through, 51
Greatness of, 313
Honored on Mercy Sunday, 89
Hymn of, 1
In Faustina's soul, 49
In the church of the convent,
570
In the vision of two pillars, 1689
Inscription on, 47
clarification of, 327
concerns about, 88
Jesus appears, as in, 1565
Jesus wants, venerated, 341
Leaflet with Image and Novena,
1255
Lord demanding its painting,
154
Manner of painting of, 49
Means of graces, 570
Obligation to paint, 154
On two pillars, 1689
Painting of, 52
Part of entire work of mercy,
154
Prayer connected with, 187
Prayerful poem on, 1
Praying for approval of, 851
Pressed to heart, 853
Printed on pamphlet, 675
Printing of, 1299
Promises attached to veneration
of, 48, 570
Promulgation of, 47
Public veneration of, 47, 414,
742
Rays of,
explanation of the red and
pale rays on, 299
extending to dying man,

with peaceful death following, 1565
from Heart of Christ dying
on the cross, 414
from Host in monstrance,
336, 344, 420, 657, 1046
from Image to Host in monstrance, covering the whole
world, 441
from monstrance, filled the
Church, 370
from Sacred Heart, 177,
1796
on Feast of The Divine
Mercy, 420
rays from the Heart, 1559,
1565, 1796
rays of love, 1370
spreading over entire world,
87
two rays from fount of
mercy, 1309
Reminder to do works of mercy,
742
Request from Jesus to paint, 1,
47
Responsibility to paint, 154
Signature on, 47, 88, 327
Signed, "Jesus, I trust in You,"
327
Source of, 47, 67
Suffering because of silence
about it, 421
Suffering over, 152
Throne of The Divine Mercy, 1
To be publicly honored, 414
Triumph of The Divine Mercy
and, 1789
Veneration of, 47, 414
source of many graces, 742
Vessel of graces, 327
Vision of,
and rays on Low Sunday,
420

comes alive, 416, 417, 851
Living Jesus looking at people, 1047
over chapel in Vilnius, 87
with votive lamps and crowds, 851
Visit to artist, 313

Intercession/Intercessory Prayer (for)

(see also **Death, Dying, Oblation, Prayers, Souls**)
All humanity, 929
Ask like a beggar, 294
At final vows, 240
Baptism, grace for Jewish lady, 916
Boldness with Jesus, 44
Certain soul, 1671
Children, 765, uphold world, 286
Chosen souls, 1703
Communion for sinners, 1806
Communion with the dying, 835
Crocheting for souls, 961
Deceased sister, 1382
Deeper knowledge of, 1077
Deeper knowledge of mercy for Father Andrasz, 1623
Dying soul, 207, 820, 924, 935, 936, 971, 985, 1015, 1536, 1639, 1684, 1698, 1777
Family community and priests, 436, 524, 845, 857, 1438
Father Andrasz, 978, 1012
Father Sopocko, 609
Feast, 1530
Friends, 1438
Girl suffering with soul, 864
Girl who needed help, but had no room, 1305
God's plan depends on persevering prayer, 872
Group of girls, 1171

Her convent, 1714
Her sister wanting to enter the convent, 982
Holy Father and priests, 925, 1501
Holy water, 602
In heaven for humanity, 930
In heaven for those on earth, 1653
Jesus asks prayers for mercy, 1070
Jesus asks prayers for sinners, 1397
Jesus, conference on, 1767
Little children, 1821
Mercy on sinners and dying, 1783
Mercy on the world, 1619
Mortification for reparation of various sins, 1248
Mother Irene, 1301
Mother Superior, 1348
New Congregation, 572
Novena for a sister to submit to God's will, 1525
Persecuted and suffering, 845
Persecutors, 1628
Pleading for mercy on the whole world, 1582
Poland, 1038 (see also **Poland**)
Power of, 202
Pray until answered, 834
Pray until at peace, 835
Prayer for dying, verified by time, 835
Praying for souls, 975
Priest, 868, 986, 988, 1607
Priests, 953, 980
Priests during Lent, 931
Priests proclaiming Divine Mercy, 1501
Refused to, because of wrong intention, 958
Request by a sister to appear to

her after death, 1615

Resolution to offer all for mercy, 861

Russia, 818

Russia and Spain, 861

Russia, Spain, Pope and clergy, 240

Sick, 1029

Sinner, 41, 987

Sinners, 908, 934 (see also **Sinners**)

Sinners of Mardi Gras, 927

Sister in need, 1518

Sister in need of change of disposition, 1527

Sister promised after death, 1614

Sister [Wanda], 202

Sister who distorts truth, 1194

Sisters, 1335

Soul in sin, 1280

Souls, 240, 621, 694, 705, 809, 996, 1375

Souls in purgatory, 748, 1185, 1186, 1723
(see also **Souls in Purgatory**)

Special graces, 599

Storm to stop, 1197

Struggle for a dying soul, 1035

Student, 1603

Suffering for dying souls, 1762

Suffering for souls, 1039

Ungrateful souls, 1538

United with the dying, 880

Wafer, 845

Whole world, 870

Work of mercy, 1401

Judgment and Urgency

(see also **Second Coming**)

Anger of God, experience of being left alone by God, 1728

Days of darkness, 83

Judgement Day, take advantage of mercy now, 1159

Judgement, never of others, only mercy, 253

Justice,
averted out of love, 570
day of mercy before, 1588
near day of, 965
only when forced to, 1588
restrained by trust, 198

Mass in homes, light from Eucharist, 991

Need of mercy, 81

Now is the time for mercy, 1448

Open floodgates of mercy, 1159

Poland and, 1533

Punishment and The Divine Mercy, 1588

Sister Faustina disarms God's anger, 1722

Take advantage of mercy while it is time, 1035

The day is near, 965

Urgency of the message, 83, 635, 848, 1159, 1160, 1588

Words of Jesus about,
coming first with mercy, 1588
lament about religious and priests, 1702
love gone from convents and churches, 1702
opening the doors of mercy first, 1146
prolonging mercy, 1160

World maintained by religious souls, 1434

Knowledge/Discernment (of)

All are as dust, 1610

All depends on God's will, 1642

Aware of a person in trouble, 1018

Bishop considering the Feast, 1463

Cross of Mother Superior, 1380

Cunning sister, 1492

Death of a sister, 973

Deceased sister in purgatory, 1382

Deceit of person, 901

Discernment of person suffering, 1031

Displeasing the Lord (mirror test of dead sister), 1383

Divine illumination filled with trust and joy, 1102

Earthly things are fleeting, 1141

Eternal destiny as a saint, 1410

Father Andrasz is pleasing to God, 1012

Father Andrasz was praying for Sister Faustina, 1529

Father Sopocko? spreading mercy, 962

Father Sopocko's work, 1472

Goal of sanctity, 1362

God, 970

God as Father at Communion, 1819

God at Communion, 1807

God, by flashes of light, 95

God gives freedom, 1135

God in one moment, 771

God, mercy, in judging, 1456

God would accomplish His work in Sister Faustina, 1477

God's anger, because of sin, 1434

God's goodness, 1607

God's holiness and our misery, 1801

God's love brings understanding of His will, 1409

Graces lavished, 1279

Graces not accepted given to others, 1294

Holy Communion remains in Sister Faustina, 1302

Humility is only the truth, 1503

Ineffective priest thinks only of himself, 1719

Innocence not lost, 1095

Interior life of God, 1102

Interior state of two, 603

Intimate knowledge of the Lord, 1049

Jesus appeared as beggar boy, 1312

Joy of heaven, from face of God, 1592

Lord's aversion for a certain soul at Communion, 1280

Lord's desire, to strive to spread the Kingdom, 1548

Malice of sin, 1334

Meeting a person with vocation, 1009

Mercy gives great joy, 1466

Mortal sin, 291

Own misery, 852

Own misery, but God's mercy, 1406

Person praying for Sister Faustina, 1018

Person with temptations concerning confession, 1736

Pierced by love and knowledge of God, 1433

Power of Chaplet for the dying, 1565

Prayer needed for dying, 820

Priest wearied from work, 1014

Sanctity, 1107

Self, 274, 1720

Self and God in silence, 1336

Sin in others by pain of stigmata, 1079

Sinners, 43

Sister not in grace, 1196

Sister wanting her own will, 1525

Sister who distorts truth, 1194

Sister who is self seeking, 1440

Sister who needs to change her disposition, 1527

Sister with distrust, 628

Some souls are called higher, 1556

Someone praying, 1455

Soul displeasing God, 1247

Soul in need, 835

Soul in need of prayer, 834

Soul in sin, 1274

Soul like a stone, 1284

Soul offending God, 987

Soul pleasing to God, 1063, 1792

Soul praying for Sister Faustina, 1419

Souls benefiting from Image, 1379

Souls in need of prayer, 828

Souls in sin cause suffering of passion, 705

Souls praying for Sister Faustina, 1444

Souls seeing snares, 1727

Souls who have aborted, 1277

Souls: wrong intention, 958

Souls' state for conversion, 1357

Speak to a certain sister, 1737

Spiritual director that would not be of help to a sister, 1223

State of a lying person, 1712

State of a soul, 1694

State of a soul of a beggar, 1283

Stigmata experienced in presence of a soul not in grace, 759 (see also **Stigmata**)

Struggle of some sisters, 1335

Suffering for a certain sinner, 1468

Transfers, 1180

True self, 1559

Two sisters, 695

Unwillingness of Lord to come to some in Communion, 1598

Visit of brother, Stanley, 1281, 1290

Women's promise to enter a convent, 396

Word to Mother General, 191

Workings of mercy, 1658

World's existence sustained by chosen souls, 1434

Life of Sister Faustina
(also see **Baptism in His Mercy, Desires of Sister Faustina, Eucharist, God's Will, Humility, Love, Mercy, Obedience, Presence of God, Saint/ Sanctity, Suffering, Transformation, Union**)

Love
(see also **Fire/Flames of Love, Mercy, Union**)

Abyss of, 1600

Alone has meaning, 502

Always, 1145

Arrow of pierced, 1082

Binds Jesus, 1193

Burns as a holocaust, 1564

Burns incessantly, 1365

Can only live in, 503

Casts out fear, 589

Changes things, 303

Compensates for the chasms, 822

Concentrated in sacrifice, 1358

Condescended to dwell in my heart, 1575

Consists in doing God's will, 616 (see also **God's Will**)

Delight to love and be loved, 1523

Demanded, 990

Desire for the world to be trans-

formed into, 1771

Desire to be transformed into, 1820

Desire to love God, 525

Doing all out of, 140

Drawn by fire of living love, 703 (see also **Fire/Flames of Love**)

Drawn into glowing center of, 1121

Drawn into Holy Trinity, 1020 (see also **Holy Trinity**)

Drew Jesus, 576

Drowned in, 1676 (see also **Baptism in His Mercy**)

Drowned in the Lord, 802

Enable me to love, 1631

Enkindle a life of love and mercy, 1365

Enkindle in the heart, 1538

Enough to know we are loved, 293

Exchange of wafer with, 1440

Fills the abyss of nothingness, 512

Fills the gap between God and creature, 815

Fire for action, 760

Flame of, 1705 (see also **Fire/Flames of Love**)

Flooded by, 994

Flows from sacrifice, 1358

For Jesus, 57

For the sake of the Lord withholds chastisement, 1489

God is, 106

God loves me, 16

God loves those we love, 1438

God loves us so much, 319

God's love and Sister Faustina's love fused, 1334

Greatest greatness, 990

Grows in us, 1191

Guide of life, 1363

Heart dies in ecstasy of, 1600

Heart filled with, 1488

Heart touched by, 946

How much God loves souls, 1073

Hymn of, 995, 1001, 1569, 1632 (see also **Hymns**)

I love You, 1323

I love You for Yourself alone, 1794

Immersed in, 1500

Immersed in God, 947

Immersed in seeing the Image, 1300

Immersed in, solves questions, 1123

In doing His will, 278

In silence, 1342

In suffering, 46

In the midst of suffering, 1239

Increases by knowledge of God, 231

Insatiable for God, 832

Intensely, 1098

Inundated in, 997

Is all sweetness and bitterness, 1245

Is the flower, mercy the fruit, 949

Jesus delighted with, 1546

Jesus loves me, 815

Jesus wants to fill with, 1017

Knows no fear, 781

Knows no obstacles, 201

Law founded on, 1478

Leads to forgetfulness of self, 1096

Love with a great love, 1372

Makes souls free, 890

Makes the soul great, 984

Measured by thermometer of suffering, 774

Meditation, 373
Mercy the fruit, 1363
Mystery that transforms everything, 890
Need to know better, 1030
Nothing can stop, 340
Nothing disturbs or stops, 1022
Of God, 296
Of God a mystery, 278
Of God is the greatest joy, 507
Of God the Creator, 702
Of God is incomprehensible, 729
Of God known in union, 771
Of Jesus in the Passion, 267 (see also **Passion**)
Of Jesus, not of new world, 587
Of Merciful Lord, 853
Of neighbor, 241
Of the heart, 1021 (see also **Heart**)
Of Trinity, 239 (see also **Holy Trinity**)
Only love satisfies, 1023
Only value, 1092
Pleases the Lord, 1489
Plunged into an ocean of, 513 (see also **Baptism in His Mercy**)
Poured into your love, 1809
Praise of, 1307
Prayer for, 94
Prayer of praise of, 1575
Prayer to surpass in, 334
Presides in union, 622
Protects the soul, 1094
Proved by gift of Son, 1584
Proved by sacrifice, 1386
Provides the gift of Eucharist, 914
Pure love capable of great deeds, 140
Purer than the Angels, 1061

Quintessence is sacrifice, 1103
Reaches God, 201
Resolution to love neighbor, 861
Set afire by Eucharist, 1769, 1807 (see also **Eucharist**)
Sister Faustina's part to love, to folly, 822
Sorrow go hand in hand, 881
Soul flooded with, 1292
Soul's greatness consists in, 889
Strengthens for great deeds, 856
Strengthened to love, 566
Suffering becomes a delight, 303 (see also **Suffering**)
Suffering go together, 843
Suffering proof of, 1662
Thermometer of suffering, 343
Transformation into, 726 (see also **Transformation**)
Transformed by, 1363, 1370
Transformed into a flame of, 1456
Transforms, 1333
True greatness, 424, 427
United to suffering, 1050
Value to God, 778
What matters to God, 997
Words are not adequate, 947
You are love itself, 1808

Mary, Mother of God
Advice of Father Andrasz to place into hands of, 1243
Advice of Jesus to ask Mary for help in temptations, 1560
Always with her, 798
Asks for prayer, 325
Bear suffering with humility, 786
Child of, at vows, 240
Close to the Immaculate Heart of Mary, 1097
Commune with God within, 454

Concern for Jesus, 1437
Consecration to Mary, 79
Day of justice, 635
Dwelling of God, 1745
Ejaculation: "Mary, unite me with Jesus," 161
Faithfully fulfill God's will, 1244
Father Andrasz's devotion to Mary, 1388
Faustina with,
at Shrine in Czestochowa, 260, 521
waiting during Advent, 792, 793
Feast of Our Lady of Mercy, 266
Feast of the Immaculate Conception, 1410, 1412 – 1415
Feast of the Presentation, 1558
Fix your gaze on the Passion of Jesus, 449
Gift of purity, 40
Guarding and instructing, 1097
Guidance, 792
Guides in decision, 1250
Hailing Mary as Mother of God, 346
Hymn to Mary, 161, 1232, 1735, 1746 (see also **Hymns**)
I am Mother of God of priests, 1585
I am your Queen and Mother, 805
Imitating Mary, 843, 1414, 1415, 1624
Instructs regarding interior life, 840
Invoking Mary's intercession, 286
Life of the New Congregation like, 625
Light from surrounds a priest, 806

Living with expectancy with Mary, 829
Mary asked to prepare for receiving Communion, 1114
Mary guides Helena, 11
Mary model of action, 1250
Model and star of life, 874
Mother of Mercy, 330
Nearness to, 1114
New Congregation should be in union with God, 625
New Congregation to prepare for the Second Coming, 625
Nothing is too much in honoring, 1413
Novena before the Assumption, 1206
Novena of a thousand Aves, 1413
Mary's intercession, 728
Offering of the flower of silence, 1105
On carrying out God's will, 449
Practice my virtues, 1414, 1415, 1416
Practice of humility, purity, and love of God recommended by Mary, 1415, 1624
Pray in the spirit, 325
Prayer for love of suffering, 315
Prayer in union with Mary, 32
Prayer of honoring, 844
Prayer to Mary, 79, 315, 844, 1469
before retreat for final vows, 220
for humility, 1306
for purity, 874
on suffering, 915
on Vow day, 240
Praying at Czestochowa, 260, 521
Preparation for the Feast of the Immaculate Conception, 1412

Prepare the world for His
Second Coming, 635
Pressed to her heart, 1415
Prolonged time of mercy, 1261
Protection of Mary, 1097
Rejoices at adoration of theHoly
Trinity, 564
Rosary, 412, 489, 515, 696, 709
Second coming, 635
Shielding us, 686
Silence of, 1398
Sister Faustina
directed to be under Mary's
care, 1243
enters convent on vigil of
Our Lady of Angels, 17
prayed to the Holy Spirit
and to Mary, 170, 1174
strengthened in suffering, 25
Speak of mercy, 635
Spoke of New Congragation and
its virtues, 1244
"Strive after silence and humility," 785
Suffering of, 915
"Take My Dearest Treasure,"
608
"Take this Most Precious
Treasure," 846
Teaches Faustina, 561
abandonment to the Will of
God, 1437
about the interior life with
Jesus,
how to live for God, 620
how to love God, 40
in Holy Communion, 840
in many things, 260
in the practice of three
virtues, 1415
spiritual life: humility, 1685,
1701, 1711
to commune with God, 454
to prepare for Christmas, 785

true love, 346
union of hearts, 786
you are my child, 1414
Tells Faustina
of New Congregation to
prepare world for the
Second Coming, 625
of the seven daggers that
pierced her heart, 786
to prepare world for the
Second Coming, 635
Time with, 840
To Father Sopocko, "Courage,"
597
Totally immersed in, 1669
Under the protection of Mary,
798
United with Jesus, 162
United with Mary, 182, 792,
1398
Vigil with Mary, 845
Visit church of the Most Holy
Virgin, 1300
Visions of our Lady
at Eucharist, 597
at Nativity, 1442
crowd of disciples, 1710
encouraging her about the
New Congregation, 449
exhorting her
to offer vows for Poland,
468
to pray for Poland, 325
Feast of the Ascension,
1711
Feast of the Assumption,
1244
Feast of the Immaculate
Conception, 564, 805, 1414,
1415
in beautiful brightness, 564
in great brilliance, 1585
in white and blue, 468
interceding for Poland, 1261

Jesus, Mary, and Joseph, 608, 846, 1442

Jesus and Mary, 88, 330, 608, 1261

at Ostrabrama, 529

in a small chapel which became a big temple, 561,

Mary and Child, 25, 529, 677, 846, 1585

Mary and confessor, 330, 597

Mary as Mother of God of Priests, 1585

of priest who loves Mary, 806

preparing her for deeper interior life with Jesus, 785

rays streaming from Her Heart, 33

visiting purgatory, 20

warning of sufferings, 316

with God, 635

with her confessor, 330

with Jesus at the Ascension, 1710

with pierced Heart, protecting Poland from punishment, 686

Words of Our Lady

courage, 597

encourage Faustina to trust her confessor, 677

"I am Mother to you all," 449

"I am the Mother of God of Priests," 1585

"I am the Mother of Mercy," 330

mystery of happiness, 346

on adoring the Trinity, 564

on compassion, 805

on humility, 1711

on suffering, 25, 316

on the sword of sorrow, 786

on the will of God, 1244

pray for Poland, 468

pray, pray, pray for the world, 325

You are my special child, 1414

Merciful Heart of Jesus (see also Love, Mercy, Union)

Agonized, 299

All hope in, 1065

Beloved peace of, 1061

Blood and water flow in Confession, 1602

Blood and water flowed for souls, 367

Brings souls to, 1209

Brother Stanley offered to, 400

Burning with love, 1142

Burns with love, 371

Call to be close to, in sickness, 797

Can do all things, 228

Can not bear ingratitude, 1537

Carried close to, 1481

Carried in, 278

Christ's desire for souls, 186

Clasped to, 928

Clinging to, 262

Close to, 229, 730, 733, 779, 1327, 1330, 1345, 1363, 1490, 1617

Comfort of, 164

Comfort to, 288

Compassion for sinners, 1521

Compassionate, 1682

Console it by accepting graces, 367

Delight of, 27, 137, 1061, 1176, 1193, 1489

Desire for 969

Desire to hide in, 1021 (see also Desires of Sister Faustina)

Meditation on, 1621

Mercy as rays, 528

Mercy gushed forth from, 832

Mercy Itself, 1777

Mercy passes through, 1309

Model of life, 167

Model your life on, 1701

Most pleasing to join suffering to His, 1513

Moved by great mercy, 282

Moved by wretchedness, 1739

Nestled close to, 1318, 1726

Never exhausted of compassion, 1827

No one ever refused, 1730

Nourishes, 465

Novena to, for brother, Stanley, 1290

Novena to The Divine Mercy, 1211, 1213, 1215, 1217, 1219-1221, 1223-1225, 1227-122 (see also **Novena**)

Ocean of mercy, 1142

Offer of treasures of, 1486

Offered self to, 668

On the paten, 239

Open, 1

Open gate to heaven, 1570

Opened as a living fountain, 1520

Opened as a spring of mercy, 1747

Opened on the cross for all, 1182

Opened with a lance, 813

Overflows with mercy, 367, 1148

Pained by mistrust after a fall, 1532

Palm Sunday, pain echoed in, 1657

Pardon for offenses to, 1144

Patron saints of, 729

Pierced by sins of chosen souls, 1702

Place in, 871

Pleased with Sister Faustina, 980

Plunge in Him, 733

Poured out, 1183

Prayer for, 650

Prayer for transformation to, 514 (see also **Transformation**)

Prayer to, 76, 187, 314

Preparation for Confession, 225

Present in, 14

Pressed to, 853, 869, 873, 1011, 1053, 1753

Priest in the, 442

Priests and religious are precious to, 531

Promised Sister Faustina will be present at Feast, 1042

Protects us from the anger of God, 1526

Rays from, 87, 177, 414, 657, 1309, 1565, 1559, 1796

Rays pass through like a crystal, 1553

Reflecting, 1542

Reflects the stirring of Sister Faustina, 1700

Refreshed by proclaiming mercy, 1521

Refreshment for tormented, 1056

Refuge in burdens, 1033

Refuge in spiritual warfare, 145

Rejoiced at purity of intention, 1566

Rejoices at return of sinners, 1728

Rejoices in Feast, 998

Rejoices in title of Mercy, 300

Resolution to unite to, 905

Rest on (near), 36, 275, 431, 498, 801, 826, 902, 929, 945, 970, 1230, 1489, 1685

Rights over, 718
Sacred Heart, 224
Sad because of no love, 1478
Sea of mercy, 1450
Seeing, 487
Shield, 465
Silent, 906 (see also **Silence**)
Sister Faustina comfort of, 580
Smuggling to, 104, 138, 96
Solace in torments, 1058
Some fill it with joy, 367
Sorrowful because of lack of understanding, 379
Soul pleasing to, 636
Source of Feast, 699
Source of "honey and milk," 1771
Source of mercy, 1190, 1507
Source of pearls and diamonds, 1687
Source of strength, 1803
Suffering from distrust, 580
Suffering from ingratitude, 580
Suffering soul closest to, 1487
Take refuge in spiritual warfare, 1287
Take treasures from, 294
Thanks for, 240 (see also **Thanksgiving**)
Throne of mercy, 1321
Torrents from, 1689
Trust in, 244, 1138
Unite self to, 873 (see also **Union**)
Virginity a flower from, 1735
Watches over, 799
Wound of mercy, 1631
Wound, pierced, source of mercy, 1485
Wounded by faults against the confessor, 362
Wounded by ingratitude, 384
Wounded by mistrust, 379

Wounded by sin, 1274
Wounded more by lack of trust than sin, 1486
You are in, 1133
You are my Heart, 1666
Your misery offered delights my, 1775

Mercy
(see also **Deeds of Mercy, Trust**)
Abandoned like a drop in an ocean of, 668
Abolishes chasm, 1692
Absolute confidence in, 1337
Abyss filled by, 1576
Abyss filled with mercy, 1576
Abyss of, 206
Accessible in confession, 1448
Act of, like to Eucharist, 285
Administrator of, 570
All enclosed in, 1076
All grace flows from, 1507
All our hope in, 681
Always forgiving, 1332
Attributes of God: holiness, justice, mercy, 180
Aware of abyss, 1131
Beg for, proclaim and glorify, 1160
Beg for self and world, 1432
Beyond imagining, 692
Beyond understanding, 631
Book written in blood contains names of souls that glorify, 689
Cannot write enough about, 1605
Canticle of, 1692 (see also **Hymns**)
Chaplet, a powerful means to obtain, 848
"Christ-Mercy," 1778
Completely imbued with, 167

Conceived in love, 651
Conference by Jesus on, 1777
Confirmed in every work of God, culminating in sinners' forgiveness, 723
Continuous imploring of, by New Congregation, 1013 (see also **New Congregation**)
Contrite souls and, 1739
Count only on, 697
Creating man out of, 1743
Creating out of, 1741
Crown of God's works, 301, 505
Cry of man in misery, 1744
Defense against just anger of God, 1516
Defense of souls, 1516
Desire to be transformed into, 163 (see also **Desires of Sister. Faustina**)
Desire to die glorifying, 1708
Difficulties will not suppress, 764
Dispenser of mercy, 31, 580 (see also **Titles**)
Dispensing, 975
Distressed have priority to, 1541
Divine Mercy will triumph, 1789
Does not reject sinners, 1122
Drawing from fountain of, 1178
Drawn only by trust, 1578
Embraces and pursues sinners, 1728
Entrusted all to, 1064
Envelops Sister Faustina, 1049
Envelops the world, 1319
Eucharist is fountain of, 1817
Even for a despairing soul, 1486
Even if a flicker of good will, 1486
Everything begins and ends with, 1506

Everything exists from, 699
Everything is the work of, 1466
Everything that exists is enclosed in, 1076
Excludes no one 1182
Exhort souls to trust in, 1567
Experience of fathomless mercy, 1073
Faustina and
    experience of the Holy Trinity, 1073
    messages from Jesus about, 1074
    "Secretary" of, 965, 1160, 1275, 1605, 1784 (see also **Titles**)
    to make known, 635
    to proclaim incessantly, 1521
    to proclaim to whole world, 1074, 1142, 1190, 1448
    to tell priests about, 177 (see also **Priests**)
    to write and speak of, 1448 (see also **Writing**)
    to write for tormented souls about, 1146
Feeling as a drop in the ocean of, 654
Few know, 731
Fills abyss, 1576
Flames, 50, 177 (see also **Fire/Flames of Love**)
Floodgates opened, 1159
Flower of love, 651
Flowing from Wounds of Christ, 1190
Flows from love, 703
Flows from the fount, Heart of Jesus, 1309 (see also **Merciful Heart of Jesus**)
For others, 163
For sinners, 730 (see also **Sinners**)

For the dying through the Chaplet, 811

Foremost attribute of God, 180, 301

Fount of, 848

Fruit of love, 948, 1363

Gazing on the abyss of, 1345 (see also **Gaze**)

Gift of purity, 1099

Glimpse of, 718

Glorifying, 163 (see also **Glorifying Mercy**)

Glory of resounding, 1659

God as, 281, 300, 1074, 1148, 1273, 1739, 1777

God does not despise the lowly, 1339

God is love and mercy, 1486

God's, 300

God's deed, 651

God's great desire to have, 1784

God's mercy, 1242 (see also **Glorifying Mercy, Mission**)

God's only motive, 1172

God's will is, 1552, 1574

Grace of conversion and perseverance, 1577

Greater than all sins, 1485

Greater than men and angels, 699

Greater than understanding of angels, 651

Greatest attribute of God, 163, 180, 301, 611, 664, 835

Greatest work, 637

Guiding thread of life, 697

Hide me in, 1480

High praises of, 1489

Holy card of Image, 711

Hour of, 1320, 1572

How few know it, 505

How great in the Incarnation, 1433

How great is God's, 1439

Hymn of, 522, 951, 1000, 1298, 1652, 1744, 1750 (see also **Hymns**)

Hymn of played, 1077

I do not fear because I know Your mercy, 1803

Immersed in the sea of, 694

Immersed self in, 1361

In creating, 85

In the Incarnation, 1433, 1745

In misery, 56, 237

In sending only son, 1745

Incarnate, 1745

Incarnation miracle and mystery of, 1584

Inciting trust in, 1582

Incomprehensible, 598, 1553

Inexhaustible, 50, 611, 631, 1273

Jesus, Love and Mercy Itself, 1074

Jesus full of mercy, 1175, 1192

Jesus on earth, 1175

Justifies and sanctifies, 1122

King of, 3, 83, 88, 367, 378

Knowledge of, 730

Knowledge of greatness of, in Cenacle, 757

Knowledge of mercy saves, 1396

Knowledge of, toward souls, 1054

Language inadequate to express, 359

Last moment of dying at, 1698

Let me enter the treasury of, 1738

Life of the soul, 611

Like a mother, 230, 249, 505

Like an ocean, 478

Litany in praise of, 949

Living fountain of, 1307

Living in peace in abandonment to, 1264

Look into the Heart of Jesus and see, 1663

Love of neighbor as Eucharist, 285

Manifold, 1313

Many souls glorifying, 1073

May all bear the seal of Your mercy, 755

Merciful Heart of Jesus a living fountain of, 1520, (see also **Merciful Heart of Jesus**)

Merciful Heart of Jesus is the throne of, 1321

Merciful Heart of Jesus is the wound of, 1631

Miracle of mercy in Confession, 1448, (see also **Sacrament of Reconciliation**)

Misery and, 718, 723

Misery cannot exhaust, 1488

Misery does not hinder, 1182

Misery not a match for, 1273

Mission to plead for, 570 (see also **Mission**)

Mother of, 330 (see also **Mary, Mother of God**)

Must pass through door of justice if mercy refused, 1146

Mysteries of, 1506

Mysteries of Divine Mercy for dying, 1684 (see also **Death, Dying**)

Mystery of, 1553, 1692, 1684

Mystery of, for the dying, 1698

Mystery of, in Incarnation, 1746

New Congregation shares in and dispenses, 539

No bounds, 718

No limits to, 1307

No moment without experience of, 697

Novena to The Divine Mercy, 1210-1230

Obtained by entreaties for the whole world, 435

Obtained by living the spirit of mercy, 550

Ocean of mercy, 718

Ocean without bottom, 631

Out of, gifts lavished, 1523

Pardons not limited, 1488

Passes into souls as sun through crystal, 528

Pierced Heart is source of, 1182 (see also **Merciful Heart of Jesus**)

Poured out from Heart of Jesus through heart of Faustina, 1777

Poured out through the Merciful Heart of Jesus, 1183

Praise of, 423, 1307 (see also **Glorifying Mercy**)

Praised by saints, 753

Praised by souls in heaven, 753

Praising at the throne, 1582

Prayer for, 819, 1570 (see also **Prayers, Hymns**)

Prayer for abundant mercy, 793

Prayer for dying, 835

Prayer for sinners, 908

Prayer for souls, 1342

Prayer for the sinner and miserable, 793

Prayer for transformation of faculties, 163

Prayer like the *Memorare*, 1730

Prayer of, 950

Prayer of praise of, 1339

Prayer to be a worthy instrument of, 783

Prayer to merciful God, 1570

Priests and, 1521 (see also **Priests**)

Priests to proclaim His mercy, 491

Proclaim it on Feast, 300
Profound knowledge of, 808, 1572
Punishment and, 1588
Pursuing a soul, 1274
Recitation of Chaplet and, 687
Reflection on, 319
Refuge behind shield of, 1488
Request of Jesus for adoration for, 1070
Rest is in proclaiming, 930
Revealed on earth, 718
Right of greatest sinner, 598
Sacrament of Reconciliation (Confession) and, 975, 1602 (see also **Sacrament of Reconciliation**)
Sea of, 178, 1520
Shield me by, 1093
Sign of end times, 848
Singing of it in heaven, 825
Singing of mercy, 761
Sinners and, 723, 1146, 1728, 1777
Sinners in most need of, 1275
Sole task of Sister Faustina's life is glorifying Souls as mirrors of, 1148
Soul filled with, 697
Souls most in need of, 1275, 1397
Souls who appeal to, 1146
Speak freely to Mother Superior, 1519
Speak to sinners about, 1396
Speak to the world of, 848
Spread the honor of, 1075
Spring of, 1747
Suffering for souls to obtain, 1399
Sung only in a small measure, 1605
Tabernacle: throne of, 1485, 1747

Take advantage of this time of mercy, 1035
Take refuge in now, 848
Teach me to open the bosom of mercy, 755
Teaching on, by a priest, 1104
Tell priest about, 177
"Tell the world about ...," 699, 1190
Thanks for, 256
Three degrees of mercy, 163, 742
Time of mercy to precede time of judgment, 83
Title of King of Mercy, 88
To be met on judgment day, 1426
To many by suffering, 1459
Today Jesus sending, 1588
Tribunal of, 975, 1448, 1485
Triumphed over justice at three o'clock, 1572
Trust in, 723, 854, 1065, 1325 (see also **Trust**)
Trust in as a child, 898
Trust in despite all, 1195
Trust in misery, 852
Trust in, peace at death, 1520
Trust in power of, 1479
Understanding of, 177
Vision of multitudes worshipping, 848
Vision of torrents from the Heart of Jesus, 1689 (see also **Merciful Heart of Jesus**)
We all need it, 1036, 1432
We all need mercy, Father Andrasz, 623
Womb of, 522, 1076, 1553
Words of Jesus,
    be merciful as I am, 1695
    conference on mercy, 1777
    from pierced Heart of Jesus,

1190 (see also **Merciful Heart of Jesus**)

His Heart as a fountain of, 1520

peace at the hour of death, 1520

write everything I tell you about mercy, 1693 (see also **Write/Writing**)

Work of Jesus, not of Sister Faustina, 1667

Work of mercy, 638

Work of redemption, 89

Works in all open hearts, 1577

Works of God and, 723

Worship of mercy through Father Sopocko, 1256

Write of, 1448 (see also **Write/Writing**)

Misery/Mercy

(see also **Baptized In His Mercy, Humility, Mercy, Sinners, Suffering**)

Abandoned, 38, 1246, 1263, 1274, 1661

Aching, 1074

Agony of soul, 43, 1662

All need mercy, 623, 1432

Anguish, 19

Black, 1

Condition of soul, 36

Darkness, 23, 73, 78, 98, 103, 378, 504, 507, 715, 1108, 1112, 1124, 1199, 1237, 1486, 1661

Desolation, 1315

Despairing, 24, 101, 522, 770, 950

Discouragement, 1086, 1487, 1488

Doubt, 40, 522, 1086

Exclusive property, 1318

Fatigue, 1065

Fear, 11, 496

Hell conspiring, 25, 41

Incertitude, 40

Lowly, 645

Mercy, Abyss of, Ocean of, 56, 66, 69, 237, 256, 320, 334, 356, 366, 382, 668, 718, 793, 852, 881, 950, 1182, 1273, 1345, 1406, 1436, 1479, 1553, 1576, 1602, 1777, 1817, 1827

Misery, Abyss of, Miserable souls, 56, 66, 69, 77, 96, 133, 174, 253, 256, 283, 320, 334, 356, 357, 361, 363, 364, 366, 382, 411, 464, 605, 606, 615, 668, 672, 718, 727, 793, 819, 836, 852, 870, 871, 881, 994, 1108, 1182, 1273, 1318, 1345, 1406, 1436, 1479, 1485, 1489, 1541, 1563, 1570, 1576, 1602, 1730, 1744, 1745, 1748, 1777, 1801, 1803, 1813, 1817, 1827

Nothingness, 91, 253, 361, 505, 512, 593, 702, 771, 947, 1237, 1436, 1558, 1559, 1743

Reflected by God, 23, 24

Sadness, 1488

Shuddered, 23

Sinner, 363, 378, 423, 522, 598, 723, 793, 1059, 1122, 1146, 1275, 1485, 1552, 1728, 1784

Struggle, 15, 615

Suffering, (see **Suffering**)

Temptation, 18

Tormented, 1138

Uneasines, 42

Unworthy, 440, 1108

Vessel, 1599

Weak, 2, 37, 247, 381, 435, 464, 495, 602, 722, 1118, 1331

Words of Faustina on her misery/mercy, 56, 66, 69,

77, 237, 256, 357, 382, 411, 423, 727, 819, 836, 852, 944, 1345, 1406, 1479, 1489, 1505, 1570, 1730, 1801, 1803, 1813, 1817, 1827

Words of Jesus on misery/mercy, 133, 378, 382, 718, 881, 944, 1059, 1074, 1146, 1182, 1273, 1275, 1318, 1436, 1485, 1541, 1563, 1576, 1602, 1728, 1739, 1777, 1784

Wretched, 237, 460, 495, 593, 836, 1243, 1417, 1489, 1739

Your exclusive property, 1318

Mission of Sister Faustina

(see also **Deeds of Mercy, Intercession, Knowledge, Oblation, Sinners, Souls, Suffering, Write/Writing, Work of Mercy**) see pp. 26-27 in *Special Urgency of Mercy,* available from Marian Helpers Center, Stockbridge, MA 01263

Begins after death, 281, 483, 570, 1209, 1729

Fears of doing, 489

Glorify mercy, 729, 1242, 1325

Here and in eternity, 483

New Congregation to plead for mercy, 570

Office and assignment to make known mercy and exhort to trust, 1567

Plead for mercy, 482

Sing of His mercy forever, 825

Task of this life and next, to exhort souls to trust, 1452

Win souls by prayer and sacrifice, encourage them to trust, 1690

You are my secretary in this life

and the next, 1605

Your assignment and duty here on earth is to beg for mercy for the whole world, 570

Mother

God addressed as, 230, 239, 242, 249, 264, 298, 505

Jesus (living Host) you are a Mother, 239, 242, 249, 264, 505

Mother Superior/General

Cross to carry, 1380

Defends Sister Faustina, 1266

General,
    care of, in suffering, 794
    New Congregation, "locks" Sister Faustina in the tabernacle, 656
    on leaving the Congregation, 1115
    visit with, 405
    word of knowledge to, 191

Get used to suffering, 700

Irene first to support sister Faustina and work of Divine Mercy, 1307

Irene shows Divine Mercy booklet, 1379

Irene spreading devotion to Divine Mercy, 1519

Joseph, advice, 222

Joseph, sharing with, 1112

Printing of Image, 1299

Reproaches Sister Faustina for being sick, 1648

Tell all to Jesus, 1162

"Things are too pretty here" (Pradnik), 1785

Troubled on account of Sister Faustina, 1348

Upgrading from, 133

Work of mercy, 1296

You catch every sickness, 1555

New Congregation

Abandonment to God's will regarding leaving, 751

Abandonment to uncertainty about leaving, 663

Act of abandonment, 1264

Admonish of illusion, 643

Advice of,
  advice of bishop, 473
  Archbishop, 585, 693
  confessor, 1117
  Father Andrasz, 506, 658, 659
  Mother General, 750

Ardor of the members, 572

Assurance that it will exist, 664, 665

At least one act of mercy a day, 1158

Begging for mercy on the world and priests, 537

Blessed Virgin Mary describes the union and prayer, 625

Cell, 565

Cell and grill, 537

Chastity, 534

Clothing of, 526

Confession, 557

Confession to Archbishop, 473

Confessor helping with, 563

Confessor says all an illusion, 643

Criteria for membership, 542

Darkness descends on decision to leave, 1115

Decision to leave present congregation, 655

Desire to do the work, 1013

Discernment to leave Congregation of Our Lady of Mercy, 1115

Dispensers of mercy, 539

Doubts about, 463

Enclosure, 554

Equality of members, 538

Faithful to order, 1130

First group intercessors, 1155

First profession, 545

Further advice of Bishop, 479

General summary, 536-573

God's will always fulfilled, 586

Holy Communion, 558

Horarium, 547

House visited, 573

Houses, 536

Humility of, 538

Income, 548

Internal suffering, 496

Jesus desires it, 437

Jesus desires to be present in the Eucharist, 570

Letters, 556

Life style of, 526

Like a beehive in the church, 664

Listening with the heart, 584

Love for souls, 539

Love for the Church, 551

Meals, 546

Mercy expressed in deeds, words, and prayer, 1155, 1158

Mission to plead for mercy, 570 (see also **Mission**)

Model on life of Jesus from crib to cross, 438

Mortifications, 565

Need of an interceding community, 623

No classes of sisters, 538

Novena to know God's will, 665

Novitiate, 544

Obedience, 535, 1650

Opposition in future, 586

Orders given that cannot be carried out, 923, 1650

Parlor, 555
Penances and mortification, 565
Possible member, 1009
Postulancy, 542, 543
Poverty, 533 (see also **Vows**)
Prayer for mercy, 537
Prayer for the Church, 551
Prayers, 547
Profession, 545
Pure and humble, 532
Purification by tensions over, 1263
Purity of intention, 550
Purpose of, 531
Push and pull of leaving, 1263
Question of leaving present community, 624
Reflection of mercy, 664
Regarding leaving the Community of Our Lady of Mercy, 449, 655, 656, 750, 1115, 1263
Relationship of sisters with the superior, 567
Relationship of the superior to the sisters, 568
Rule of,
    silence, 552, 553
    speech, 553
Satan's attacks, 540, 644 (see also **Spiritual Warfare**)
Second group: prayer and works of mercy, 1156
Shares in and dispensers of mercy, 539
Sharing about details, 1090
Silence, 552, 553
Small communities, 536
Spirit of,
    humility, love and poverty, 550
    mercy, 551
Spirit of the convent without

Sister Faustina, 892
Strength given to do the work, 527
Struggle of leaving Congregation of Our Lady of Mercy, 449, 1263
Submitted to confessor, 1117
Suffering because of, 786, 1176, 1263
Suffering over the tensions of leaving, 1263
Sweet to live and die in, 322
Talking to Jesus about, 1090
Tension of knowing God's will, 624
Tension over fulfilling God's will, 615, 1650
Third group, prayer and deeds, without vows, 1157
Three levels, 1155
To entreat mercy for the world, 585
To mediate between heaven and earth, 438
To obtain mercy by entreaty, 435
To plead for mercy, 435, 1013
To proclaim and obtain mercy, 436
Union with Jesus, 572
Uniqueness of each soul, 568
Vision of the convent, 892, 1154
Vision of disrepair of convent, 559
Visit from a possible member, 993
Visit with the Archbishop, 585
Visiting a possible site, 573
Will intercede for mercy, 664
Will make mercy their own attribute, 664
Will of God made known, 615
Will reflect God's greatest attribute, 664

Words of Jesus on,
>"fear nothing," 665
>leaving the community, 776
>mission of the New
>Congregation, 570
>obedience, 1650
>pleading for mercy, 531
Work, 549
Year of postulancy, 543
Zeal of, 572

Novena (for)

Before Feast of Mercy, 1059,
>1209-1229
Before OSTRA BRAMA, 528
Booklet printed, 1379
Conversion of the world, 1059
Divine Mercy,
>First Day, for all, 1210
>Second Day, priests and
>religious, 1212
>Third Day, devout and faith-
>ful souls, 1214
>Fourth Day, pagans, 1216
>Fifth Day, heretics and
>schismatics, 1218
>Sixth Day, the meek and
>humble, 1220
>Seventh Day, those who
>glorify mercy, 1224
>Eighth Day, souls in
>Purgatory, 1226
>Ninth Day, lukewarm souls,
>1228
Establishing Feast, 1041
Father Sopocko asks for the text,
>711
Intentions, hymns, and prayers
>of the Novena before the
>Feast, 1209-1229
Leaflet printed, 1255
Of Chaplets, 476, 851
>before Feast of Mercy, 796
>to obtain Divine Mercy for

Poland, 714
Of prayer, "O Blood and
>Water..." 33 times for Holy
>Father, 341
Poland, 59, 1251 (see also
>**Poland**)
Pope, 341
Promise of all graces, 796
Thousand Hail Marys, 1413
To Divine Mercy, 1209-1229
To Holy Spirit to inspire Pope
>about the Feast, 1041
To see Father Sopocko, 1257
To see Father Sopocko for work
>of mercy and for Poland,
>1206
To the Heart of Jesus, 1290
Words of Jesus about Novena
>before the Feast, 1059

Obedience

>(see also **Vows**)
Always, 624
Command to write, 1006
Counsel of Father Andrasz, 506
Do what it allows, 1650
Grace for, 1401
Greater reward in, than
>penances, 933
How good to obey, 1686
In the New Congregation, 535
In trial, 99, 102
Jesus obeyed, 535
Needed to please God, 354
Not mortification, 28
Opportunity for sacrifice, 1386
Oranges eaten out of, 1023
Power of, felt over sickness,
>1378
Power of, for souls in Purgatory,
>1187
Saved by, in dark night, 1112
Saving in trial, 105

Sharing with a sister about, 1594

Takes away weakness, 381

To confessor, 139, 639, 1374

To doctor and confessor, 894

To Mother Superior On not attending dying, 924

To spiritual director, 910, 932, 979

To the Lord and to confessor, 645

To the rule, 189

Torture of tension over, 981

Vow and virtue, 93

Wins souls, 961

Writing under, gives glory, 1567

Oblation/Holocaust (for) Victim-Offering

(see also **Souls, Suffering: for Sinners**)

Act of, 309, 726, 1264

Atonement: powerful in union with Christ, 482

Calls for free consent, 135, 136

Final breaking of her will, 309, 726, 923, 1264

Immediate experience of effects, 311

Permission for, 311

Self and misery, 1318

Self for sinners, 80, 1680

Self to be a priest and missionary, 302

Three intentions: spread of mercy, sinners and dying, person in charge, 1680

Total offering of self, 309

With Christ in atonement, 482

Passion

(see also **Stigmata, Suffering**)

Book of love, 304

Experience of, 203, 705, 931, 1016, 1028, 1060

on seeing a sinner, 291

thorns, 41, 349, 1399, 1425, 1619

torture and love, 1056

scourging, 614

stigmata, 942, 976, 1079 (see also **Stigmata**)

with Christ, 646

with Jesus in Gethsemane, 1558

Experienced,
   at Mass, 1663
   during Holy Hour, 384

Felt at Communion, 808

Felt Christ's wounds, 1646

Felt for a dying soul, 1724

First experience of stigmata, 759

Five wounds, 1055

For a girl in need, 1305

For souls, 1627

In the garden and in prison with Jesus, 1054

In the whole body, 1627

Invisible stigmata, 964

Invoking in prayer, 72

Jesus scourged, 526

Jesus thirsting, 583

Lesson of humility, 184

Martyrdom, 304

Meditation on, 267, 369, 618, 661, 737, 1184, 1621, 1625

Meditation on, gives graces, 737

Pain, 1010

Passion, 203, 705, 931, 1016, 1028, 1060

Reflection on, 267 (see meditation , above)

Scourging, 188

Scourging, crowning with thorns, 408

Sea of mercy, 948

Seeing a sinner, 291

Seeking light and strength in, 654

Spent night in prison with Jesus, 1515

Stigmata, 942, 976, 1079 (see also **Stigmata**)

Thorn(s), 41, 349, 1399, 1425, 1619

Torture and love, 1056

Vision of, 639, 736, 737 (see also **Vision of Jesus**)

Vision of, on Good Friday at three o'clock in 1936, 648

Vision of scourging of Jesus and experience of, 614

With Christ, 646

With Jesus in Gethsemane, 1558

Peace

At the hour of death, 810, 1520, 1541

In trusting in God's mercy, 300, 699

Words of Jesus, "snuggle close to My merciful Heart" for peace, 1074

Penance

(See **Sacrament of Reconciliation**)

Places

Calvary Shrine trip cancelled, 64

Cracow, return to (on May 11, 1936), 655

Cracow, return to, from Rabka, 1207

Czestochowa, first visit, 260

Czestochowa, visit to, 521

Home,
blessing by parents, 402
brother Stanley offered to the Heart of Jesus, 400
example of father's prayer, 398
growth of children, 399
joy of arriving, 397

prayer for sisters, 401
tears after leaving, 403
visit to parish, 400
visit with dying mother, 395
visits of friends and children, 401

Pradnik,
a cell like a Carmelite, 799
arrival at (April 1938), 1675
departure for final stay, 1674
feeling better, 897
men's ward, 803
return after Christmas, 849
return from (3/27/37), 1066
return to convent for Christmas, 844
sickness is grave, 1679
visit of Sister with lemons, apples, and tree, 842
visit with apples and greetings, 816

Rabka,
darkness of soul on departure for, 1199
leaving early for, 1198

Vilnius,
adapting to new house, 265
arrival, 261
garden work, 262
leaving for, with the Lord, 259
Ostra Brama, Image displayed, 89

Walendow,
April (1936), 653

Poland

Anger of God and chastisement of, 1533

Bless her, 286

Blessed Virgin Mary asks for blessing, 1585

Chastisement of Poland, a
mercy, 1533
From her the spark that will prepare the final coming, 1732
Jesus: for your sake I will bless
the entire country, 39
Jesus: I bear a special love for
her: a spark will come from
her, 1732
Novena for, 39, 59, 714, 1251
Prayer for, 39, 286, 468, 686,
1188
Sacrificing for, 1038

Prayers (for) (to) (of)
(See also **Novena, Prayer/
Monologues, Spiritual Life**)
Abandonment, 569
Asking Mary for help, 1114
Atonement, 320
Blessed Virgin Mary (see also
Mary, Mother of God)
for courage in suffering, 915
for protection, 874
prayer to, 170
Calls for perseverance and
patience, 147
Calming a storm, 1197
Chaplet, 475, 476 (see also
Chaplet)
Chaplet against a storm, 1731,
1791
Chaplet for rain, 1128
Chaplet for the dying, 1565
"Close to Your Heart," 1726
Communion, transform me,"
1826
Confessor-Director, 127
Conversion, "O Blood and Water
...," 187
Conversion of sinners, 741
Courage in fear, 859
Creator hidden in the Eucharist,
1692

Desire for others' sanctity, 1581
Desire to love, 288
Destroy self-love, 371
Divine Mercy, 1005 (see also
Mercy)
Dying sister, 314
Effort and grace, 1696
Enlightenment, 410
Eucharist, 223, 356, 1350, 1733
(see also **Eucharist: Prayer**)
Eucharist for mercy, 1751
Eucharist, Jesus as Friend, 877
Eucharist, support in suffering,
1484
Every grace comes through, 146
Experience of being prayed for,
1444, 1455
Experiencing flashes of light, 95
Extolling God's majesty, 440
Faculties to be transformed into
mercy, 163
Faithfulness to, despite dryness
and temptations, 872
Father Andrasz, 1388, 1623
Fear only to offend You, 571
Feast, 1003
Finding light and strength in,
166
Friends, 1438
Gifts of the Church, 1759
Glorifying mercy, 836, 1584
God's greatness and my
wretchedness, 1417
God's will, 328, 497, 688, 832,
1265
Grace to carry out retreat resolu-
tions, 376
Graces to be faithful, 1265
Hail to You, Jesus, 1575
Healing, 1089
Holy Hours of Intercession, 356
Holy Spirit, 170
Holy Spirit, Blessed Virgin

Mary, guardian Angel and patrons, 1174
Holy Spirit for the retreat, 1174
Honoring Blessed Virgin Mary, 844
Humble prayer disarms anger, 320
I love You, 1323
I trust in Your mercy, 101
In convent, 19
In praise of mercy, 423
In spirit always, 325
In suffering, 195, 382
In weakness, 66
Increase your mercy, 950, 951
Infant Jesus, 845
Inspired by God, 1593
Interceding for a sister with a novena, 1525
Interceding for community, family and the world, 857
Interceding for family and Church, 346
Interceding in union with the Eucharist, 1501
Intercession, 20, 396, 599, 809
Intercession after death, 1614
Intercession by crocheting, 961
Intercession for,
    convent, 1714
    dying, 971, 1035
    dying soul, 820, 1015, 1639, 1698
    dying this day, 873
    dying, until peace, 835
    Father Andrasz, 978, 1012
    Feast, 1041
    happy death, 985
    Jesus in Eucharist, 80
    mercy, 996
    Poland, 1038
    Pope, 925
    priest, 823, 868, 986, 988, 1014
    priests, 953
    sisters, 1335
    soul, 685, 1671
    souls in purgatory, 1185, 1375, 1723
    souls of sinners, 975
    superiors, 1348
    world, 870
Intercession in union with all the Masses, 1783
Intercession through the Image for a dying woman, 916, 917
Intercession until a soul is at peace, 828
Intercession with discernment, 958
Interior and exterior difficulties, 147
Involves the whole person, 1103
Jesus as model, 1351
Jesus be patient with me, 366
Jesus for help, 264
Jesus, have mercy, 53, 118, 119, 869
Jesus, I trust in You, 162, 249
Jesus, Mercy, 162, 869
Jesus our defense, 1535
Jesus, save me! 644
Jesus source of life, 1490
Jesus to judge her work of mercy, 660
Joy in God's will, 1403
Just as I am, 1734
King of my heart, 1811, 1812
Know God alone, 338
Knowledge of God, 483
Knowledge of self, 297
Life of love and of mercy, 1365
Life of the spirit, 1344
Life, way and truth, 298
Light, 410
Light and strength in affliction,

Like Jesus in the garden is pleasing, 1534

Listening, 725

Litany of the Eucharist, 356

Litany, mercy in praise, 949

Live in the present moment, 1183

Living host, 1826

Living victim, 908

Lonely heart, 247

Longing and suffering, 25

Longing for God, 469, 501, 1365, 1573, 1600, 1721

Longing for the coming of the Lord, 854

Longing with suffering, 867

Love, 94, 507

Love of God, 1756

Love of neighbor, 1769

Love of the Eucharist, 1771

Love of the Trinity, 525

Martyr of inspirations, 497

Mary and offering, 79

Mary, for courage in suffering, 915

Mary, for purity, 874

Mary in suffering, 315

Mary on Christmas, 844

Meditation, prepared by the Lord, 149

Merciful God, 1570

Merciful Heart, 76, 692 (see also **Merciful Heart of Jesus**)

Mercy, 3, 24, 361, 423, 428, 651, 697, 727, 793, 819, 950, 1093, 1122, 1307, 1553

Mercy and misery, 363

Mercy and not anger, 1526

Mercy at hour of death, 813

Mercy for sinners, 72, 793, 908, 914

Mercy for the dying, 835

Mercy hidden in the Eucharist, 1485

Mercy in misery, 366

Mercy in times of difficulty, 1065

Mercy of the Trinity, 617

Mercy on all, 836

Mercy on the sisters, 383

Mercy on the world, 473, 1582

Mercy poured out on us, 1339

Mercy through the Heart of Jesus, 1183

Mother of God, 170

Native country, 286

Need for, in spiritual warfare, 146

Need of sinners, 349

Night spent in, 662

Novena for a certain soul, 364 (see also **Novena**)

Novena for the Pope, 341

Novena of Chaplets, 851 (see also **Chaplet**)

Novena of a thousand Hail Mary's, 1413

O Blood and Water, 84, 187, 309, 341, 813

O God of great mercy, 1570

O Great God, 288

O wound of mercy, 1631

Oblation as victim, 1264

Oblation for Feast, sinners and work of mercy, 1680

Offering of Jesus to the Father, 648

Offering of sacrifice, 1342

Offering of self, 1318

Offering of suffering, 740

One another, 1171

Only recourse in difficult times, 1387

Perseverance in, 157, 860

Person in need, 396

Pleasing God, 1493
Poland, 39, 286, 468, 686, 1188 (see also **Poland**)
Praise in suffering, 70
Praise of God's glory, 1708
Praise of God's mercy, 1007, 1590
Presence, 691
Priest interceding, 1529
Priest praying, 1534
Priests, 491, 1052
Protection, 76
Protracted suffering, 1795
Pure love, 371
Purity, 79
Rays of mercy come through the Heart of Jesus, 1553 (see also **Merciful Heart of Jesus, Rays**)
Reliance on the Lord, 91
Relief from heat, 701
Resolution to pray for Russia and Spain, 861
Rosary, 412, 489, 515, 696, 709
Routine, 62
Russia, 240, 818, 861
Saint Joseph, 1203
Seeing God's glory, 419
Shielded by mercy, 1480
Sinners, 72, 80, 186, 350 (see also **Sinners**)
Sister in purgatory, 58
Someone praying for Sister Faustina, 155
Souls, 599 (see also **Souls**)
Souls in purgatory, 516, 519, 1426 (see also **Souls in Purgatory**)
Spain, 240, 861
Spiritual Communion, 80, 81
Storm, ceased after, 1197
Strength, 495
Strength in weakness, 1344, 1630
Submission to divine pleasure, 440
Suffering for Christ, 1662
Support by the Mother Superior, 1266
Support in the struggle, 1606
Support of sisters by letters, 1673
Surpass all in love, 334
Thanks for all, 724 (see also **Thanksgiving**)
Thanks for graces and blessings, 1794
Thanks for knowledge of misery, 363
Thanks for suffering, 343, 1616
Thanksgiving for the congregation, 1291
Three o'clock, 1319 (see also **Hour of Great Mercy**)
Time of dying, 813 (see also **Death, Dying**)
To be faithful to grace, 716
To be merciful, 163, 755 (see also **Deeds of Mercy**)
To do God's will, 492, 1360 (see also **God's Will**)
Transform my heart, 514 (see also **Transformation**)
Transformation, 1289
Transformation of heart, 514, 832
Transformation to be living sacrifice, 908
Transformed into, 996
Trinity, 5, 163 (see also **Holy Trinity**)
Trust, 24, 25, 317, 746 (see also **Trust**)
Trust in darkness, 73
Trust in mercy, 69
Trust in mercy during suffering, 1489 (see also **Suffering**)

Trust in suffering, 23, 697, 1418
Trust in turmoil, 1195
Union with God, 503 (see also
    Union)
Vocations, 1290
Welcome, 1731
Will of God, 650
Words of Jesus about praying for
    a student, 1603
Work of mercy, 638 (see also
    Works of Mercy)
You alone are good, 1800
Your will be done, 78, 328, 503,
    615 (see also **God's Will**)

Prayer/Monologues

(see also **Hymns, Prayers,
    Spiritual Life**)
Abiding in God, 478
About leaving for the New
    Congregation, 751
Acceptance of all, 485
After Communion, 1385, 1386
Asking strength in offering suf-
    fering, 1740
Attachments, 338
Canticle of love, 989
Child, 264
Child of the Father, 242
Childlike simplicity and love,
    334
Church, 197
Concern for souls, 929
Confession, 377
Consecrated like the Eucharist,
    for mercy on the world, 1564
Consoling Jesus, 284
Constant vigil, 1340
Deeds of mercy, 1269
Desire and love of God, 507 (see
    also **Desires of Sister.
    Faustina**)
Desire to be Eucharist, 641, 832
    (see also **Eucharist**)

Desire to be a great saint, 1372
Desire to be a missionary, 302,
    303
Desire to be a Saint, 1333 (see
    also **Saint/ Sanctity**)
Desire to hide in Christ, 591,
    592, 593
Discovering Jesus, 766
Doing God's will, 957
Dying souls, 1015 (see also
    Dying)
Edginess, 275
Eternal light, 830
Father, 240
Favor of vows, 220
Focusing on Jesus, 804
Glorifying God's mercy, 1242,
    1691
God is King; I a beggar, 199
God's goodness, 460
God's goodness and trust, 386
God's way, 422
God's will, 667, 1356 (see also
    God's Will)
Goodness of God in creating
    angels, 1741
Greatness of God's mercy, 1584
    (see also **Mercy**)
Guard me Jesus, 1764
Hidden, 306
Hiding in His mercy, 791
Holy Communion, 1392
How loved a suffering soul is by
    God, 963
Humiliations, 243
Humility, 1306, 1436
I am weak, God is strong, 602
Intercession for a sister, 1518
    (see also **Intercession**)
Intercession for lukewarm souls,
    1703
Intercession for souls, 1249
Intercession for the dying, 880

Jesus and the foundation of sanctity, 1331

Jesus guide me, 1118

Judgment, 1470 (see also **Judgment**)

Judgment by God and by others, 1456

Keep me close, 298

Know God better and so love Him more, 1030

Knowledge of misery, 256

Knowledge of self, 297

Lament, 200, 1161

Last day of life, 825 (see also **Death**)

Life offered in suffering for others, 1580, 1581

Longing for God, 761, 841, 885, 969, 970, 1473 (see also **Desires of Sister Faustina**)

Longing for God and souls, 1366

Longing for heaven, 899

Longing for Jesus, 918

Longing for souls, 235

Love, 195, 778-782 (see also **Love**)

Love and mercy of God, 1523

Love as a child, 230

Love in suffering, 227

Love of Christ suffering, 267

Love of God, 296, 340, 815

Love of suffering, 276

Love of Trinity, 283

Majesty of the Trinity, 576

Mary, 240 (see also **Mary, Mother of God**)

Mercy, 357, 611, 631, 859, 898, 1178, 1466, 1506, 1507, 1553, 1803

Mercy in misery, 237, 668, 1332, 1730

Mercy Incarnate, 1745

Mercy toward mankind, 1743

Mistrust, 287

Mystery of God, 73

Name of Jesus, 862

Night prayer, 679

Novitiate of Jesus, 228

Obedience, 376

Offering as victim of love, 239 (see also **Oblation**)

Offering of her heart, 1064

Offering suffering with Christ, 1574

Ordinary day, 245

Peace in God's mercy, 1345

Power of love, 889, 890

Power of sacrifice, 482

Praise of mercy, 917, 1749 (see also **Glorifying Mercy**)

Praise of the Divine Madman, 278

Redeeming man, 1747

Repentance, 1562

Request for enlightened mind, 1474

Retreat, 218

Sacrifice, 954

Secrets of the heart, 201

Sickness and death, 1729

Sister Faustina's mission of mercy, 1325 (see also **Mission**)

Solitary soul, 247

Solitude with God, 1395

Souls in purgatory and those suffering, 692

Speaking the truth, 1482, 1483

Starting an eight day retreat, 1326 (see also **Retreat**)

Steeped in thanksgiving, 1367-1369

Strength to suffer for souls, 1613

Striving for love of God, 1245

Struggle with sickness, 1314

Submission in suffering, 1204

Submission to mercy in suffering, 1449, 1450

Suffering, 208, 209, 224, 253, 351, 782, 831, 896, 1071, 1208 (see also **Suffering**)

Suffering with Christ, 1656

Talking to Jesus, 670

Tension of weakness and desire, 760

Thanks for book of the Passion, 304, 305 (see also **Thanksgiving**)

Thanks for suffering, 343

Thanks to Jesus for visiting during solitude, 1062

Thanksgiving, 1001

Thanksgiving for God's love, 1285

Three requests at perpetual vows, 240

Transparency to God, 1336

Trust, 357, 358, 761, 1138 (see also **Trust**)

Trust and love, 1371

Trust and mercy, 505, 1234

Trust in the Eucharist, 1239

Union of hearts at perpetual vows, 239 (see also **Union**)

Union with Jesus, 832, 1145

Unveiling God's mercy, 930

Value of sacrifice, 482

What displeases God, 273

When oversensitive, 783

Will of God, 952

Your will be done in suffering, 1237

Preaching of God's Mercy

Exhortation of Jesus to Faustina about the, 164, 300, 687, 1074, 1142, 1190, 1396, 1521, 1665, 1666

Graces promised to proclaimers, 377, 378, 379, 1075, 1540

Insufficiency of, 1273

Priest and, 50, 570, 1521 (see also **Priests**)

Presence of God

Almost constant, 890

At midnight Mass, 846

Awareness of, removed, 1181

Before retreat for final vows, 220

Communion, 846

Envelops, 629, 635, 715, 808, 1109

Enveloped and transpierced, 983

Experience of, 40

Immersed in, 143

In the churches, 409

In a spiritual and physical way, 747

Jesus is always present, even in battle, 1499

Live in, 1560

Mystery of His Essence, 911

Not felt during Holy Week, 413

Of God floods the soul, 512

Of God on Easter (1936), 649

Of God's majesty, 491

Of Jesus pervades, 574

Of living God, 844

Of Trinity, 486 (see also **Holy Trinity**)

Penetrates, 480, 627

Penetrates as the sun through a crystal, 1814

Pervades, 702, 969, 1391

Physical and felt presence, 1821

Piercing like the sun, 946

Resolution to practice presence of God, 861

Soul filled with, 708

Suddenly invaded, 26

Through the day, 1781

To the humble, 1605
With fire, 490 (see also
  Fire/Flames of Love)
Wrapped up in, 1410

Priests
(see also **Confessor, Spiritual
Director**)
Asked to preach on mercy
  (1937), 1072
Blame of spiritual director's and
  confessor's imprudence, 937
Blessed Virgin Mary: "Tell the
  priests what you have seen,"
  1585
Day offered for, 823
Dear to the Lord, 988
Desire to be and how she can be,
  302
Examine Sister Faustina's writ-
  ing, 1045
Give power to, 1052
Give us holy priests! 941, 1052
Great intimacy with Jesus, 1240
How much is demanded of you,
  941
In need of prayer, 986
Inexperienced, 595
Interceding for, 934 (see also
  Intercession)
Interceding for during Lent, 931
Jesus in white garment, 459
Jesus shared power and mystery
  with, 1240
May mercy be with them, 1052
Need of those who can love,
  1014
Power to those who proclaim
  mercy, 1521
Prayer like Jesus in the garden,
  1534
Protect them, 1052
Reverence for, 953
Suffer for the work of mercy, 838

Test souls, 595
To tell everyone of mercy, 570
Wearied by work, 1014
Words addressed to priests by
  Jesus, 50, 177, 570, 687,
  1521
Words of Mary to priests, 1585
You are bright candles, 75

Promises
(see also **Chaplet, Feast, Hour
of Great Mercy, Image, Mercy,
Novena, Trust, Work of
Mercy**)
Before day of justice, the day of
  mercy, 1588
Chaplet, mercy at death, 687
Chaplet, mercy for the dying,
  810, 811, 1035
Chaplet, mercy in life and death,
  754
Chaplet, mercy to hardened sin-
  ners, 687
Feast, Confession and
  Communion for complete for-
  giveness, 699
Feast, last hope of salvation,
  965, 998
Feast, remission of sin, 300
Graces to those who trust, 1074
Great trust, no limits to generos-
  ity, 1602
Image, a vessel of mercy, 327
Image, rays shield, 299
Image, victory over enemies, 48
No limit to generosity to a
  repentant soul, 1728
Novena (of Chaplets) every pos-
  sible grace, 796
Peace in trusting, 300, 699
Peace to those who come to
  mercy, 1074
Prayer, "O Blood and Water,"
  186, 187

Prayer for sinners is always answered, 1397

Proclaiming mercy, grace and protection, 378

Proclaiming mercy, mercy at death, 379

Proclaimers of mercy, shielded at death, 1540

Sinners turning to mercy, graces and justification, 1146

Sinners who trust have greatest right to mercy, 1541

Spread devotion, I will supply what you lack, 1074

Spread devotion, protection in life and death, 1075

Three o'clock, nothing refused, 1320

Three o'clock, obtain everything, 1572

To priests, hardened sinners will repent, 1521

To those who trust, greatest sanctity, 1784

Trust in mercy, all will be drowned in mercy, 1059

Trust in mercy, peace at death, 1520

Trust in mercy, will not perish, 723

Trust in mercy, will obtain mercy, 420

Trusting soul, embraced by mercy, 1777

Trusting soul, the Lord will care for it, 1273

Purgatory
(see **Souls in Purgatory**)

Radio
Hymn of love, 994

Hymn swept into God, 997

Psalms sung by priests, 1061

Silence lost by, 837

Rays
(see also **Image, Merciful Heart of Jesus**)

Bathing in, 697

Change the world, 1000

Crystal, pass through Merciful Heart like, 1553

Divinity radiates through the soul, 1336

Enveloped by, during stigmata, 759

Extend over the whole world (1935), 420

Filled with, 1488

From the Eucharist, 344, 370, 420, 441, 657, 1462 (see also **Eucharist: Rays from**)

From the Heart of Jesus, 87, 177, 414, 465, 836, 1559, 1565, 1796

From the Host, 336, 344, 441, 657, 1462

From the Host into hands of clergy, 344

From the Host to the world, 1046

From the Image, 1, 47

From the Image, pierce the hearts of people, 417

From the Image, pierced the Host and to the world, 441

From the monstrance, 370

From the open wound of the Merciful Heart of Jesus, 1309

Heart of Mary, 33 (see also **Mary, Mother of God**)

Influence the soul to bear fruit, 605

Let rays of grace enter, 1486

Meaning of, 299

Mercy from the heart, 528

Of love, 104

Of mercy enter a heart ajar, 1507

Of mercy from Christ's side, 648

Of truth, 727

Over the world, 83, 87

Pass through Merciful Heart of Jesus like a crystal, 1553

Pierced her heart, 439

Prayer for enlightenment, 852

Prayer to envelop non-believer, 780

Prayers for rays of mercy, 514

Shelter of, 299

Show up what displeases God, 71

Striving to be transparent like a crystal, 805

Trusting souls will radiate to others, 1074

Upon entire human race, 72

Religious Life

(see also **New Congregation, Spiritual Life, Virtues, Vows**)

Call for faith, 253, 352

Call of Jesus, 9

Catechism of vows and virtues of poverty, chastity and obedience, 93

Command of directress, 24

Community life, misunderstandings, 720

Darkness, 27

Early vocation, 7

Effect of pride, 1170

End of the novitiate, 26

Fasting: assigned as portress, 530

First vows, 27

Habit, 22

Humiliations, 151

Jesus is novice master, 228

Knowledge of God's will, 354

Novitiate begins, 21

Obedience, 376

Obedience in mortification, 28

Observing the rule, 189

On envy, 833

Our Lady of Mercy Congregation, 322

Patience, 179

Permissions monthly, 246

Probation, call to final vows, 165

Rule, grace to follow, 306

Rules,
> not kept, 266
> resolutions, 226
> silence and, 226

Rumors, 123, 125, 128

Stirred by renewal of vows, 1780, 1781

Suffering, 19, 22, 387

Suffering caused by sisters, 1268

Suffering from sisters, 149, 165, 168, 181, 182, 196, 1194, 1241

Temptation to leave, 18, 19

Third probation, begun with tears, 178

Under obedience to write, 1568

Union with souls, 391

Vocation to Our Lady of Mercy, 14

Vow form, 248 (see also **Vows**)

Words of Jesus, vows and rules, 1763

Zeal for souls, 350

Resolutions

(see also **Retreat: Resolutions**)

For Lent (of 1937), 934

For the year (1937), 163, 861

Mortification, 246

Resolutions, 246

Reviewed for the year (1936), 162

Retreat(s)

Annual retreat (of 1934), 273, 274, 275

Anticipation, 214

Before final probation, 169

Before final vows, 218

Before final vows, a promise of help, 213

Before perpetual vows, 167, 169-178

Cancelling self-will, 371

Chart of victories and defeats, 1352-1355

Concluding thoughts (on eight day retreat), 1370

Conclusion of three days led by Jesus, 1779

Confession, 174, 175

Confessor will answer doubts, 169

Directed by Jesus, 1752-1780

Eight day retreat, 371-394, 489-505, 725-744, 1326-1372

Examine chart, 1352, 1353, 1355

Fight for the glory of God, 1548

For hospital attendants, 974

God uses the weakest, 464

Graces prepared by Jesus, 167

Guidance of the Spirit, 1326

Ignation, 251

Insights, 274

Jesuit retreat in private, 251

Jesus asks about, 295

Jesus deals with a perfect soul, 1359

Jesus directs, 229

Jesus speaks through the priest, 456

Monthly retreat, 855, 1145, 1174, 1178, 1394

Mortification, 246

One day, 787, 855, 903, 974, 1621 (on the Heart of Jesus)

One day (January 30, 1938), 1548

One day . . . on God's mercy, 998

One day retreat of suffering, 1204, 1205

Outlines by Mother Joseph, 217

Patrons, 728

Peace given by the Lord, 169

Permission to make the three day retreat, 1752

Prayer for, 273

Preached by priest from America, 172

Priest confirms Sister Faustina, 461

Reassured by confessor of her spiritual path, 174

Resolution, silence and union, 905

Resolution, union with Christ, 1177

Resolution, union with "Christ-Mercy," 1778

Resolution, union with God and silence, 1105, (see also **Resolutions**)

Resolutions, 176, 241, 246, 274, 375, 504, 790, 905, 1105, 1177, 1352

Resolutions, after perpetual vows, 241

Resolutions, on silence, faithfulness, thanks for suffering, 743

Resting with Him in her heart, 903

Retreat before perpetual vows, 218-239

Satan's temptations, 173

Thirteen resolutions: one day retreat, 861

Three day retreat, 456-469, 1101-1108

Three day retreat directed by the Lord, 1709, 1752-1779

Three lights, 274

Transformation by love, 1363, 1370 (see also **Transformation**)

Union with Jesus, 467

Sacrament of Reconciliation (Confession)

(see also **Confessor**)

Advice of Jesus
   for souls who wish to benefit from, 113, 132, 1784
   to Faustina on, 1602, 1725

And Feast, 699 (see also **Feast**)

And Merciful Heart of Jesus, 225 (see also **Merciful Heart of Jesus**)

Angel cannot absolve, 1667

Beg for God's mercy, 1432

Chaplet for penance, 847

Choosing what humiliates, 225

Condition for receiving mercy and forgiveness, 300, 699, 1108

Fountain of mercy, 1602

Healing and education, 377

Is different for spiritual guidance, 654

Jesus is present, 466

Jesus speaks through the priest, 763

Joy after retreat master's advice, 175

Meeting place of Jesus and souls, 1602

Mercy drawn by trust, 1602

Miracle of Divine Mercy, 225, 1448

No need to confess before every Communion, 1611

Obedience, 628

Of a ward as a sign, 74

Permission for penance, 1347

Prayer for priests, 637

Prayer for the confessor, 647

Praying for sinners not to fear, 975

Preaching about Divine Mercy and, 1521

Priest acts in place of Christ, 331

Priest is a screen for Jesus, 1725

Reveal all, 232

Soul set free, 234

Tempted not to go, 1802

To Father Andrasz, 55, 233

To Father Andrasz before Vilnius, 257

To the chaplain, 1469

Too weak to give account of her soul, 1637

Tribunal of mercy, 975, 1448 (see also **Tribunal of Mercy**)

Trust and, 1602

Unable to open up, 496

Vision of Jesus, 817

Words to the penitent, 113

You are on the way to salvation, 1205

Sacred Scripture

As Job, friends abandon in suffering, 1509

Behold, I come to do your will (Heb 10:7), 830

Be merciful (Lk 6:36), 1695

Being in agony, he prayed more earnestly (Lk 22:44), 157, 872

Communing with Angels (Mt 18:10; Ex 23:20), 1200

Do not fear; I am with you (Mk 6:50), 129, 613, 797

Do with me as you please (Lk 1:38), 136

Drinking the cup of God's will

(Mk 14:36), 343

Dying thief on the cross (Lk 23:39), 388

Even if you kill me, I will trust (Job 13:15), 77

Eye has not seen (1Cor 2:9), 777

Gazing on Jesus (Heb 12:2), 1351

Go out into the whole world and teach in My name (Mt 28:18-20), 1710

God disciplines those He loves (Heb 12:6), 1253

God has prepared marvels (1Cor 2:9; 2Cor 12:1-7), 160

God strips the soul He loves (Heb 12:6), 1259

Holy, Holy, Holy (Is 6:3), 1741, 1805

I live in Him and He in me (Gal 2:19), 318

I thirst (Jn 19:28), 583, 648

In You I can do all things (Phil 4:13), 954

Incomprehensible mercy of God (Rom 11:32-36), 492

Jesus desires to pour divine life into souls (Rom 5:5), 1784

Jesus in the Gospel is model, 510

Jesus is meek and humble of Heart (Mt 11:28-29), 526

Jesus is the way, the truth and the life (Jn 14:6), 298

Letter itself does not make love grow (2Cor 3:6), 1637

Love casts out fear (Jn 4:18), 589

Love and prayer for those who cause suffering (Mt 5:44), 1628

Love is capable of great things (1Cor 13:4-13), 140

Love never ends (1Cor 13), 1022

Love of God in spirit and truth (Jn 4:23), 1270

Magnificat said in suffering (Lk 1:46-55), 68

Meditation on,
    Baptism of Jesus, 365
    John 15, 1757
    John 19, 1765
    John 21, 1773
    Jonah, 331
    the Passion, 369, 618

Merciful according to His mercy (Ps 51), 611

Nothing will separate us (Rom 8:38-39), 340, 947

Of yourself you can do nothing (Jn 15:5), 639

Out of your mouth I judge you (Lk 19:22), 854

Passion is Christ's book of love, 304

Prayer in the Garden of Olives (Mt 26:39), 1394

Prayer in Gethsemane (Mk 14:36), 157

Rejoicing with those who rejoice (1Cor 13:6), 633

Resurrection after a share in passion, 205

Review of the past year with scriptural ejaculations, 162

Satan is the father of lies (Jn 8:44), 1405

Snatched up to the throne of God (2Cor 12), 474

Some live by the letter (2Cor 3:6), 1478

Soon in my Father's house (Jn 14:2), 1616

Souls fill up suffering of Christ (Col 1:24), 604

Speaking the truth (Eph 3:5), 1482

Suffer with the suffering (2Cor 11:29), 481

Suffering of present compared to glory (Rom 8:18), 605

Watch (Lk 21:36; Mk 13:33), 639

Whatever good you do, is done to me (Mt 25:31-46), 1029, 1768

When I am weak, then you are powerful (2Cor 12:10), 1655

Word of God living (Heb 4:12), 135

You found none to console (Ps 68:2), 1609

Your will be done (Mk 14:36; Lk 22:42; Mt 26:42), 615, 1487

Saint/Sanctity
(see also **Desires of Sister Faustina, Fire/Flames of Love, God's Will, Graces, Heart, Humility, Love, Obedience, Presence of God, Transformation, Union**)

Close union of will with God's will, 1107

Desire to be, 1326, 1332, 1333, 1361, 1362, 1363, 1372, 1410, 1571, 1581, 1650, 1718

Jesus: "You are that saint," 1650

Knowledge of, 1410

Related by Saint Therese, 150

Resolution to become, 1361

Sisters talk about, 1672

Souls, Sanctified "if only", 1682, 1684, 1784

Useful to the Church, 1030, 1364, 1475, 1505

Vision of pleading to Sister Faustina, 31

Saints
(see also **Visions, General: Saints**)

Jesuits in heaven, 683

Reflect a virtue — Sister Faustina glorifying mercy, 1242

Saint,
    Andrew Bobola, account of canonization, 1650
    Barbara, vision of asking for Novena for Poland, 1251
    Claude de le Colombiere, and Gertrude as patrons, 728
    Ignatius, vision of, 448
    Ignatius, his rule is adaptable, 448

Saint Joseph,
    at Nativity, 1442
    urging devotion, 1203
    vision of, 608

Saint Therese, of the Child Jesus, a dream, 150

Saint Vincent de Paul, God's hand when things are impossible, 1189

Second Coming
(see also **Judgment and Urgency**)

Blessed Virgin, Faustina and, 635

Deeds of mercy and, 1158

Hymn of, 1589

Nearness of, 965

Prayer of Faustina for, 1570

Preparation for, 1155

Signs of,
    days of darkness, 83
    Divine Mercy preparation for, 848, 1146, 1588

Words of Jesus, the spark from Poland will prepare for, 1732

Silence
About interior experiences, 680

And the rule, 226

And union with God, 477

Before the Blessed Sacrament, 73

Before those who do not acknowledge truth, 1164

Better to judge self, 1336

Communicating without words, 560

Constant watch, 1340

Conversation with the Lord in, 137, 1718

Describes union with God, 767

Engulfed her soul, 1333

Favored by Jesus, 739

Full of love, 1342

God is displeased with talkative soul, 1008

Happiest moments, 289

Holy Spirit speaks in, 552

How precious in sleep area, 1476

I desire solitude, 432

I will sing of my suffering by, 1490

Immitating Blessed Virgin Mary, 1398

Importance of, 118

In difficult moments, 944

In recollection God speaks, 452

In suffering, 126, 236, 487, 896, 1040, 1656

In the refuge of the Merciful Heart of Jesus, 1033

In time of torment, 1119

Jesus: "...My voice, which is so soft that only the recollected souls can hear it," 1779

Laid at feet of Mary, 1105

Language of God, 888

Language of Love, 1489

Long talks with the Lord in, 411

Lost by radio, 837

Needed in spiritual warfare, 145

Of the heart, 185, 726

Of the Heart of Jesus on the cross, 906

Prayed without words, 154

Resolution to, 743, 790, 861, 905

Respect for rule of, 375

Response to Satan, 1497, 1498

Response to storms, 792

Retreat resolution, 743, 1777

Struggle to keep, 171

Submission to will of God in, 1200

Suffering in, 70

Sword in struggle, 477

To hear God, 118

To hear the voice of the Holy Spirit, 1828

Tongue, 118, 119

Transforming, 682

Undisturbed by suffering, 1022

Unending delight in, 407

With certain person, 277

Sinners

(see also **Intercession, Intercession for Souls**)

All suffering for, 1637

Can reach greatest sanctity "if only" they trust, 1784

Cannot escape God, 1728

Compassion for, 1521

Desire conversion of, 1489

Draw mercy upon, 1777

Great right to mercy, 598

Holy Hour for, 319

If only they knew mercy, 1396, 1397

Immersed in mercy, 206

Jesus asks for help to save, 1645

Mercy of Jesus for, 1665

Miracle of mercy restores in Confession, 1448

Needs only set his heart's door ajar, 1507

Not to fear God's mercy, 1059

Novena First day for sinners, 1210

Offering of self for, 80

Poor if shut the door, 1507

Prayer and suffering for, 1783

Profiting from suffering, 1468

Pursued by mercy, 1728

Receive peace by the Chaplet, 1541

Sorrow of Jesus in the Garden, 1507

Suffering and interceding for, 927, 1428, 1622, 1640

Tell them of my mercy, 1666

Souls

(see also **Intercession, Mission, Prayers, Souls in Purgatory**)

All daily action deposited in the Church for, 1505

All for, 1549

All graces from fount of mercy, 1190

Begging mercy for, 996

Bound closely in heaven, earth and purgatory, 594

Christ yearns for souls, 206

Converted by Sister Faustina, 640

Crocheting for, 961

Day to day martyrdom saves, 1184

Desire for, 235, 1489, 1645

Deceased Sister, 594

Draw all, 1466

Dying in need of prayer, 1015

Emptying of self for, 224

Experience of thorn for, 1425

Give me souls, 1426

God's love for, 245

Holy Water, 602

I live for, 382

Imploring mercy, 1574

Increase my heart for, 692

Interceding for, 692

Jesus help me save souls, 1797

Joy in graces for, 579

Joy of saving, 641

Like a corpse, 1448

Live to bring to mercy, 971

Lord desires perfection of, 1601

Must pay off each debt, 1375

Need of suffering to save, 1612

Offering for, 243 (see also **Oblation**)

Penance and prayers for, 685

Prayer and sacrifice, 745

Prayer and suffering for, 709, 735

Prayer for, 599, 694, 1375

Prayer for a Jewish lady, 916

Prayer for mercy, 1342

Reparation for, 619

Suffering for, 740, 842, 875, 943, 953, 1010, 1032, 1062, 1263, 1435, 1622 (see also **Oblation, Suffering**)

Suffering for dying, 1762

Suffering stigmata for, 759, 1468 (see also **Stigmata, Passion**)

Sweet toil, 450

Thousand saved by prayerful meditation, 1783

What are you doing for, 1184

Writing for, 1471

Souls in Purgatory

(see also **Dying, Intercession**)

Do God's will, 518

Enter often, 1738

Eucharist, Mass offered for, 21

Happiness and God's will, 515

Intercession for a sister, 1382

Intercession for a soul, 1185-
1187, 1375
Mary visiting, 20
Prayer for, 1426, 1723
Request for a Mass for, 21
Request for prayer, 516, 519,
1723
Sister in, 594
Suffering for a soul, 1186
Three sisters leaving, 748
Vision of, 20, 412
Visit of sister, 973

Spiritual Direction
(see also **Confessor, Father
Andrasz, Father Sopocko,
Spiritual Director**)
Direction, 937-941

Spiritual Director
(see also **Confessor,
Sacrament of Reconciliation**)
Away at time of turmoil, 1118
Desire to be steeped in thanks-
giving, shared with, 1368
Examine for attachments, 337
Gift of, 331
Grace of, 721
Great grace, 1561
Jesus asks for boundless sinceri-
ty with, 1561
Jesus is director, 670
Lack of, 108
Obedience to, 979
Should be holy and experienced,
939
Should test obedience, 939
Thanks for, 749, 981
To be prayed for, 938
To confirm God's guidance, 939
Value of, 749
What a grace, 968
Would be more saints if more
saintly confessors, 940

Spiritual Life
(see also **Desires of Sister
Faustina, Eucharist,
Fire/Flames of Love, Gems of
Sister Faustina, Glorifying
Mercy, God's Will, Graces,
Heart, Humility, Hymns
Love, Mercy, Obedience,
Prayers, Prayer/Monologues,
Presence of God, Religious
Life, Silence, Spiritual
Director, Stigmata, Suffering,
Thanksgiving, Trust,
Transformation, Union,
Virtues , Vows**)
Abandoning self to God's will,
1169, 1437
Acceptance of joy and suffering,
485
Accepting God's grace as He
sends it, 715
Admonishment to follow inner
convictions, 1383
Adoration in dryness, 268
Advice of Father Andrasz, 55
Advice of Father Andrasz on
times of dryness, 1243
Advice of Father Sopocko on
humility, suffering and
patience, 270
Advice of Jesus on response to
spiritual warfare, 1760
Advice of superior about confes-
sor, 1162
All in God's will, 1642
Always a novice, 265
Asking questions, 560
Assurance of superiors, 222
Attachments, 337
Attention to inspirations, 1464
Attributes of God, 180
Aversion for sin, 1334
Awareness of God, 887
Awareness of God's greatness,
702

Awareness of heaven, 1439

Battle of life, 606

Beauty of surroundings does not lessen the sacrifice, 1785

Before important actions, 1549

Being a royal child, 992

Being faithful to prayer, 872

Being faithful to the Holy Spirit, 1556

Bilocation, to pray for a dying man, 1798 (see also **Bilocation**)

Call to sacrifice as victim, 135

Caution by spiritual director on sudden visions, 1068

Celebrating the Jubilee Year, 250

Channel of mercy, 636

Charity to the sick, 1268

Chart of examen and victories, 1352-1355

Chastity, 534 (see also **Vows**)

Childlike response, 1726

Childlike simplicity, 332, 333, 334, 921

Childlike, of Saint Therese, 56 (see also **Saints**)

Comfort from Confession, 1469

Comfort in prayer, 860

Command of directress when in despair, 24

Communing with the Heart, 1021

Communion as strength, 1826

Communion with God, 461, 603

Community life, 1126

Complete trust in The Divine Mercy, 1679 (see also **Trust**)

Confession, 225 (see also **Sacrament of Reconciliation**)

Confession and obedience, 628

Confessors and Confession, 112

Confirmed in purity, 1097, 1098

Consent to suffering in atonement, 190

Considering eternal life, 1550

Constant vigil, 1340

Continuous striving, 1548

Conversing with Jesus, 610

Conviction of attaining sanctity, 1362

Cooperation with grace, 204, 271, 1258

Cross and suffering, 1112

Daily sacrifices, like flowers, 208

Dark night of the soul, 23-27, 94-146, 1558, 1559 (see also **Dark Night of The Soul**)

Darkness, suffering, 24 (see also **Suffering**)

Darkness and temptations, 77

Darkness of soul after admonition, 644

Decisions made in good conscience, 800

Deeds and feelings, 663

Degrees of knowledge of God, 605

Denial of self will, 375

Dependence on the confessor, 670

Desire, for a saint in the congregation, 1650 (see also **Desires of Sister Faustina, Saint/Sanctity**)

    for God, greater than for food, 1026

    for sanctity, 1505

    for silence in the sanatorium, 837

    to be a saint, 1333, 1372 (see also **Saints**)

    to suffer, 853

    suffering (see also **Suffering**)

Despair, trial of trials, 98 (see

also **Dark Night of The Soul**)

Devotion to God's mercy, 745 (see also **Mercy**)

Devotion to Saint Joseph, 1203

Difference between Confession and spiritual direction, 653, 654

Difficulty of community life, 720

Discovering Jesus in difficult people, 766

Discretion of the Lord, 1615

Distrust, 595, 698, 731 (see also **Trust**)

Divine guidance, 1250

Divine illuminations, 1102

Divine Presence, 26, 27, 432, 649, 747, 983, 1109, 1330, 1391 (see also **Presence of God**)

Divine Presence on hearing a hymn, 994

Do not build up difficulties, 788

Doing God's will delights the Trinity, 955, 956, 957

Doing the will of God, 800 (see also **God's Will**)

Dryness, advice on weakness, littleness, faithfulness and obedience, 1243

Effects of oblation as victim, 311

Effort of union with God, 1595

Emotions in suffering, 1152

Envy, 833

Essence of virtue is the will of God, 678

Eucharist offering, 483

Evaluating all by God's ways, 766

Exercise of heroic virtues, 758

Experience of God's love, 1104, 1121 (see also **Love**)

Experience of union with Jesus, 1090 (see also **Union**)

Faith, 210 (see also **Trust**)

Faithful in darkness, 1235

Faithfulness in dryness, 1246

Fast of seven days, 530

Fear of God, 732

Fear, responding as a child, 290

Feast of the Church, 481

Feeling of being apart, 744

Feelings during suffering, 1628

Fighting off Satan, 1496-1499 (see also **Spiritual Warfare**)

Fix our eyes on Jesus, 1483

Following Christ: like Head, so body, 1580

Following the Holy Spirit, 148 (see also **Holy Spirit**)

Forgiveness, 390, 632, 1148

Free consent to victim offering, 136

Free will spurning God's love, 580

Freedom under direction, 142, 144, 145

Fruits of labor, 1402

Gazing on the merciful Heart, 906 (see also **Gaze, Merciful Heart of Jesus**)

Gift of inner peace, 674

Gift of knowledge, 1719, 1720 (see also **Knowledge**)

Gift of knowledge about her brother, 1281, 1290

Gift of peace, 1134

Gift of souls, 1277

Glorifying God versus glory of self, 1149

Goal of man, 1329

God alone is enough, 454

God cares for us, 922

God defends us, 600

God dwelling in the heart, 785,

God is love, 729 (see also **Love**)

God is merciful, 1131 (see also **Mercy**)

God strips those he loves, 1259

God uses our prayers, 621

God withdraws all externals, 149

God works in stages, 1478

God's goodness, 458

God's grace in temptation, 1086 (see also **Spiritual Warfare**)

God's love and the will of God, 1409

God's love touching the heart, 946, 947

God's presence, 491, 574 (see also **Presence of God**)

God's will, 251, 666, 667, 775, 787, 1365, 1394, 1504 (see also **God's Will**)

God's will always, 374

God's will and our labors, 952

God's will and suffering, 1625

God's will in life and death, 897, 898

God's will in suffering, 794, 795

Grace for suffering illness, 1341 (see also **Graces**)

Grace of a spiritual director, 721, 749

Grace of an ordinary day, 244

Grace of innocence of Sister Faustina, 1095

Grace of intimacy, 1019

Grace of union with God, 767-773 (see also **Union**)

Graces by inspiration and enlightenment, 392

Graces for the dying, 1684

Graces given because of humility, 1099 (see also **Humility**)

Graces not used, 1294

Graces unexpected, 158

Greater knowledge of God, the stronger is love, 974

Greatness in self knowledge, 900

is in great love, 984

Greatness of our destiny, 1410

Growth through interior suffering, 981

Gulf between us and God, 199

Heart a dwelling for Jesus, 193 (see also **Heart**)

Heart wounded by love, 943

Hearts fused into one, 1024 (see also **Union, Heart**)

Hiddeness, 255

Holiness and the Holy spirit, 291

Holiness attained by good will, 291

Holiness is union with God, 1107

Holocaust of the will, 923 (see also **Oblation**)

Holy Spirit as spiritual director, 658 (see also **Holy Spirit**)

Holy Trinity, 30 (see also **Holy Trinity**)

Horror of sin, 1016

Humiliations, 128, 129, 133

Humility, 55, 464, 1092, 1436, 1502, 1503, 1605 (see also **Humility**)

Hypocrisy, suffering caused by, 1579

Illusions, 130, 131, 143

Imitation of Mary, 843, 1398, 1415, 1624 (see also **Mary, Mother of God**)

Immersed in love of God, 1123, 1500 (see also **Baptism in His Mercy**)

Insignificance of the human brain, 1527

Inspiration of the Holy Spirit, 359 (see also **Holy Spirit**)

Inspirations avoided, 130

Inspirations submitted to confessor, 139

Instructed by Our Lady on interior life, 840 (see also **Mary, Mother of God**)

Intention of love, 822

Intention of souls, 619

Intention valued by God, 822

Interior suffering, 1785

Intimate union with God, 622 (see also **Union**)

Jealousy, 633

Jesus,

    and the foundation of sanctity, 1331

    in details of life, 360

    is teacher of mystery, 824

    speaks with a despairing soul, 1486

    speaks with a perfect soul, 1489

    speaks with a sinful soul, 1485

    speaks with a soul striving for perfection, 1488

    speaks with a suffering soul, 1487

    suffered for everything, 149

    uses confessor, 145

Joy at graces, 1049 (see also **Graces**)

Joy, my heart trembles with, 1824

Joy in silence, 407 (see also **Silence**)

Joy in suffering, 303

Knowledge (see also **Knowledge**),

    about a certain confessor, 1423

    of God, 95, 1133

    of God's graces,, 1279

    of heaven, 1592

    of misery, 256

    of self, 852

Lack of awareness of the presence of God, 1181

Lack of religious spirit, 1139

Lapses into vice opposed to desired virtue, 1087

Leaving all to God, 1179

Led by God's spirit, 293 (see also **Holy Spirit**)

Led into the unknown, 910

Let your rays nourish me, 465

Life dull but a treasure, 62

Life is passing, 1141

Life like a garden, 296

Life of prayer, suffering and work, 1545

Listening with the heart, 584

Live to bring mercy to souls, 971

Living a life of faith, 1549

Living in God, 478

Longing for God, 16, 26, 27, 57, 469, 470, 807, 850, 856, 885, 918, 952, 1026, 1137, 1303, 1710 (see also **Desires of Sister Faustina**)

Lord delights in a pure heart, 1706

Lord's mysterious ways and suffering, 1656

Loss of grace by grumbling, 690

Love, 140, 389, 502, 513, 1172 (see also **Love**)

Love alone, 373

Love and sorrow, 881

Love and suffering, 279, 1050

Love drives away fear, 589

Love in suffering, 784 (see also **Suffering**)

Love is in God's will, 279

Love is the greatness of the soul,

997

Love of God, 292, 815, 1755

Love of God grows, 1191

Love of God strengthens the soul, 1094

Love transforms, 889, 890, 1363

Major grace tested by patience, 1084

Mary as teacher, 620

Meditating on the Passion as mortification, 618

Meditation on the Passion, 369, 1621 (see also **Passion**)

Meditation of the Passion leads to humility, 267

Mercy flows from love, 703

Mercy in deeds, words, and prayers, 1155-1158 (see also **Deeds of Mercy**)

Mercy is the fruit of love, 1363-1365

Mercy toward sinners, 1274

Minor transgressions like moths, 306

Mission of mercy after death, 281

Moments of talking to the Lord within, 1793

Mortification and obedience, 183

Mortification and the Passion, 369

Mortification during Lent, 934

Mortification, iron belt, 183

Need of confessor/spiritual director, 35, 97, 98, 108, 111, 115, 121, 122, 127, 131, 132, 139, 141, 142, 331, 937-941 (see also **Confessor, Spiritual Director**)

Need of divine light in spiritual conversations, 1495

Need of humility, 55 (see also **Humility**)

Need of mercy at death, 1673

Need of peace, 145

Need of prayer, 146, 147

Need of prudence, 1106

Need of recollection, 452

Need to exercise the heroic virtues, 758 (see also **Virtues**)

Need to follow interior inspirations, 756

New Congregation general summary, 536-573 (see also **New Congregation**)

Night of prayer on the Passion, 661

Not acting on our own, 1790

Obedience, 376, 535, 624, 1594, 1686 (see also **Obedience, Vows**)

Obedience demanded, 28

Obedience gives strength, 1378

Obedience in darkness, 68

Obedience in suffering, 105

Obedience to superior's order [do not attend the dying], 924

Oblation of self, 309 (see also **Oblation**)

Offering of little things, 961

Openness with spiritual director, 680

Ordinary days, 1373

Patience, 607, 632, 1514 (see also **Virtues**)

Patience with neighbor, 1376

Paying little attention to the senses, 1270

Peace from God's will, 1328

Peace in suffering, 455

Peace in the battle of life, 1173

Peace of soul, 792

Penance of refusing oranges vs obedience, 1023

Penitent, 113

People do not know how to perceive the soul, 1445

Perfection is union with God, 457

Permission for mortifications, 932

Permission for special penance, 1347

Permission for the act of oblation, 311 (see also **Oblation**)

Pleasing God, 380, 411

Poverty, 533 (see also **Vows**)

Power of obedience, 1187

Power of sacrifices with love, 1316, 1317

Practice of Mary's virtues, 1624 (see also **Mary Mother of God**)

Pray for your confessor, 647

Prayer (see also **Prayers, Prayer/ Monologues**)

Prayer break, 226

Prayer in difficulties, 166

Praying, 1524

Preparation for death during retreat, 1343

Preparation for Holy Communion, 1804-1828

Preparation for Mary's Feast, 1412

Preparing as for death, 1551-1552

Presence of a living flame of love, 1776 (see also **Fire/Flames of Love**)

Presence of Eucharist, 318 (see also **Eucharist**)

Presence of God, 346, 411, 486, 582 (see also **Presence of God**)

Presence of God in praying, 577

Presence of God in the heart, 582, 903

Presence of the Trinity, 451, 911

(see also **Holy Trinity**)

Presence with the heart, 797

Pride, 1170

Proof of love through sacrifice, 1386

Pure intentions, 484

Purification by tensions over the New Congregation, 1263

Purpose of life, 729

Reflection on vows, 254

Rejoicing at others, graces, 579

Relationships, 695

Relief of suffering in prayer, 792

Remorse for repeated error,1293

Reparation for sin, 1248

Repentance, 388

Repentance on meditating on the Passion, 1766

Resolutions for the year, 162 (see also **Resolutions**)

Resolutions of silence, serving and trust, 504

Resolutions on silence, faithfulness and suffering, 861

Response to adversities, 509

Response to grace, 120 (see also **Graces**)

Response to spiritual warfare, 1287 (see also **Spiritual Warfare**)

Resting on the Heart of Jesus, 801 (see also **Merciful Heart of Jesus**)

Results of tribulation, 115 (see also **Spiritual Life: Need of confessor/spiritual director**

Rose buds, all difficulties offered to Jesus, 1823

Routine, 508

Rule of love in desolation, 1315

Sacrifice makes souls useful, 1358

Sadness from repeated falls, 1488

Salvation of souls, 735 (see also
    Souls)
Sanctity to be useful to the
    Church, 1364 (see also
    Saint/Sancticity, Mission)
Seeing God in everything, 148
Seek God within, 454
Seeking God in adversities, 511
Seeking Jesus in the Gospel, 510
Self-denial and the will of God,
    462 (see also **God's Will**)
Self-will crossed out, 374
Sentence from Saint Vincent de
    Paul, 1189
Silence, 118, 226, 277, 682, 905,
    905, 906, 1119 (see also
    Silence)
Silence in suffering, 487, 1200
Silence is a sword, 477
Silence is God's language, 888
Silence needed for, 1672
Sincerity of relationship with
    sisters, 1440
Singing of a canary, 907
Small things and the will of
    God, 1262
Solitude, happiness in, 1395
Solitude, hymn of, 1699
Spend your life doing good, 55
Spiritual childhood, 56, 332-335,
    921, 1481, 1726
Spiritual marriage, 912, 1020
    (see also **Union, Fire/Flames
    of Love**)
Spiritual suffering, 615 (see also
    Suffering)
Starved relationship, 901
Striving for holiness, 1475
Struggle with temptation of fear,
    1704
Struggles before receiving a
    grace, 1100
Submission to God, 734

Sudden lights, 733
Suffering the Passion with Jesus,
    1054-1058
Suffering with Christ, 669
Suffering with Jesus, 1508, 1509
Supremacy of love, 778, 779
Surrender to God's holy will,
    1679
Sustained by grace, 480
Take heed of interior inspira-
    tions, 756
Taken into the Trinity, 1670 (see
    also **Holy Trinity**)
Teaching by Blessed Virgin
    Mary on humility, 1711
Teaching by Jesus on, 1685,
    1687, 1688, 1701
Tears of sorrow, 1781
Tears over the Passion, 977
Temptations and darkness, 96,
    97
Temptations of oppression, 673,
    674
Tepid and self-concerned, 1284
Thanks for suffering, 724
Thanksgiving for grace of purity,
    1096
Thanksgiving to God, 855
Three degrees of God's will,
    443, 444
Times for ardent prayer, 1387
Times of darkness, 1120, 1124
Trial of trials, complete aban-
    donment, 98-111 (see
    also **Dark Night of The Soul**)
Trial of trials, obedience, 96-100
    (see also **Dark Night of The
    Soul**)
Trials sent by God, 96
Trials sent to those loved by
    God, 96
Trials work of Satan, 96 (see
    also **Spiritual Warfare**)
Trinity, 472 (see also **Holy**

Trinity)
Trust, 1400 (see also **Trust**)
Trust during darkness, 78
Trust during torments, 681
Trust in God's mercy, 1406
Trusting during desolation, 944
Truth speaking out, 1482
Types of visions, 882-884
Union of hearts, 1056, 1057
Union with God, 582, 883, 884, 891, 1135 (see also **Union**)
Union with Jesus, 467
Union with the Trinity, 1129 (see also **Holy Trinity**)
Union with the Trinity on the Feast, 1073
Use of time, 351
Value of confessor, 257 (see also **Confessor, Spiritual Director**
Value of humiliations, 593
Value of sacrifice, 482
Value of suffering, 342-343
Victim souls support the world, 926
Vision of Jesus scourged, 639
Vow of chastity, 16 (see also **Vows**)
Will of God, 372, 374, 375, 603, 652, 724, 725, 821, 1101 (see also **God's Will**)
Will of God and sorrow, 886
Word of knowledge, 1712, 1736, 1737
Word of knowledge about a soul, 1792
Words of Jesus on (see also **Words of Jesus,** on related topics),
    conference on mercy, 1777
    considering the passion, 1761, 1762
    conversing in the heart, 581

desiring the perfection of souls, 1601
directing of souls, 1784
Eucharist, 1770
hour of death, 1539
humility, 1293, 1361
illuminating the world by chosen souls, 1601
ingratitude, 1537
interior life, 1685, 1701
love of neighbor, 1768
need of silence, 1008, 1717
perfection, 1165
practice of humility, purity and love, 1779
purity of intention, 1566
responding to temptations, 1560
sacrifice and prayer, 1767
sanctification, 1682
trust in mercy, 1784
vows and rules, 1763
Yielding to others, 789
Zeal for souls, 350

Spiritual Warfare

Adversary afraid to quarrel with a soul full of love, 1643
All falls before God's power, 858
Appearance of cat, 412, 873
Appearance of Satan, 520
Attack against a priest, 1384
Attack of absurd thoughts, 607
Attack of black figures, 323
Attack of dislike for the spiritual, 1405
Attacks by discouragement, 129
Attempts to hinder work of mercy, 1659
Battle in old age, 517
Children in need of defense, 765
Conference by Jesus on, 1760

Continuous fight, 1287
Daily battle, 606
Demons as dogs, 320
Demons block the way, 418, 419
Demons fleeing at prayer for the dying, 1798
Demons form human hearts, 418
Doing battle, 509
Enemy crushed, 480
Evil spirit could not stand offering of suffering, 1464
Fall of angels, 1332
Feels God's power in, 1583
Felt hostility, 1646
Five directives from Jesus on spiritual warfare, 1560
Followed by peace and joy, 499
Fortified by Communion, 1823
Fortified by Jesus, 1630
Frightful temptations, 1558
Fruit of the battle, 499
Fury of Satan, 713
God strengthens, 1086
God turned his gaze from rebellious angels, 1339
Hated by evil, 706
Help of Guardian Angel, 419
Holy water, 601
Hurled flower pot, 411, 412
Hymn, 1742
In old age, 517
Inner peace in attack is a grace, 674
Jesus: be like a knight in battle, 1823
Jesus: I am always with you, 1499
Look to God who fights, 1720
Looking for an ideal soul, 1127
Lucifer knew but did not do God's will, 666
Malicious figures surround sister, 416

Mercy of God will triumph, 1789
Mocking of Satan, 644
Multitude of demons block the way, 418
Name of Jesus is victorious, 873
Need for prayer, 146
Need for spiritual director, 145
Power of God defends in, 1799
Power of holy water, 601
Praise of mercy makes Satan flee, 378
Prayer for grace in, 783
Ready to battle, 890
Refugee in Merciful Heart of Jesus, 1033, 1287 (see also **Merciful Heart of Jesus**)
Response of silence, 1497
Satan,
   disturbs peace, 1802
   do not pray for the Feast, 1497
   do not pray for sinners, 1405, 1465
   do not tell your confessor about your soul, 1497
   do not tell sinners to trust, 1497
   do not write about the goodness of God, 1138
   grinds teeth and bangs things, 1583
   hates Father Sopocko, 1384
   hates mercy, 764, 812, 1167, 1583, 1659
   looking for idle souls, 1127
   mocking regarding New Congregation, 644
   never speak of God's mercy, 1497
   opposes works of mercy, 812, 1115
   speak no more of this mercy of God, 1405

threatens the New Congregation, 540

throws a flower pot, 411

under the guise of a poor soul, 520

vanished at the sign of the cross, 1405

wants self-directed people, 938

Satan admitted that God's mercy is persecuting him, 1167

Satan can wear the cloak of humility but not obedience, 939

Satan crying out, "Do not write," 1338

Satan defeats the proud, 450

Satan's anger at works of mercy, 1583

Satan's anger at writing on mercy, 1583 (see also **Write/Writing**)

Satan's attack while writing on mercy, 713

Satan's hate for mercy, 764, 812, 1659

Satan's hate of mercy and Sister Faustina, 412, 418, 419, 1167, 1646

Shaking of bed, 412

Shielded by the wings of God, 1799

Spirit fled for dying man on saying the Chaplet, 1798

Standing up to evil, 686

Strength from Eucharist, 91

Strengthened for combat, 145

Struggle of light and dark, 307

Suffering and prayer shackled Satan and snatched souls, 1465

Suffering of abandonment, 496

Temptation against the confessor being human, 173, 1715

Temptation not to form the New Congregation, 540

Temptation not to go to Confession and Communion, 1802

Temptation to discouragement, 129, 1497

Temptation to illusion, 173, 359

Temptations of Satan about the work of mercy, 96-97, 1405, 1496-1499 (see also **Work of Mercy**)

Temptations to blasphemies, 673

Torment stopped by presence of Jesus, 674

Trials from Satan, 96-97

Trust and, 723

Trust and vigilance, 606

Trust during, is power, 823

Trust grows, 761

Turning souls from hell, 639

Ugly sight of Satan, 540

Victory of mercy, 1789

Vision, Satan as a cat, 412, 873

Vision of black figures, 323, 873 (you torment us in hell)

Vision of dogs, 320

Vision of hell, 741

Voice of evil spirit, "Do not pray for sinners," 1464, 1465

Watchfulness, 145

We are at war, 145

Weapon of mercy, 745

Where Satan cannot harm director, he uses people, 1384

Words of Jesus,
    at a conference, 1760
    Satan gained nothing by tempting, 1499
    Satan's hate, 412

Stigmata

(see also **Passion, Suffering**)
Because of soul in sin, 1247

Experience of, 976
Experience of wounds, 1646
Five wounds, 1055
For a sister, 1196
Invisible but painful, 964
Pain of, because of sinner, 1079
Pain of Passion, 942
Suffering for a dying person, 1536
Suffering for souls, 759
Thorns for a soul, 1425

Suffering(s)
(see also **Health/Illness, Intercession, Oblation, Passion, Stigmata**)
Abandoned to the will of God, 134, 1648
Abortion, sin of, causes violent suffering, 1276, 1277
Accomplishing duties during, 70
Accusations, 200
Act of love in physical weakness, 1085
Act of oblation as victim, 309, 1264
Adding external sufferings, 117
Advice of superior, 68
Advises about a sick sister, 1651
After the trial, 104
Against hope, 386
All for souls, 953, 1647
Allowed by God, 106
And peace, 1394
Angels would envy Holy Communion and suffering, 1804
Anguish of the mind, 496
Are daily bread, 145
Armed with patience and silence, 209
As a perfect holocaust, 923
Asked for healing as a sign of God's will, 1091

Asked for share in Passion, 1034
Asking for strength, 1740
Almost to death, 696
At ingratitude, 698
At sight of suffering, 1039
Aware and preparing for Holy Communion, 717
Bearing another's temptation, 192
Because image could not be explained, 421
Because of sinners, 1274
Because of work of mercy, 966, 1531
Beloved is hidden, 1120
Blindness during, 109
Body is crumbling, 1616
Brought mercy to many, 1459
Burden with, 1113
Burning in love, 351 (see also **Love**)
But an opportunity for virtue, 1268
But gazing faithfully at the Lord, 1239
Buys souls, 324 (see also **Souls**)
Call to, 135, 308, 309
Care of Mother General, 794 (see also **Mother Superior/General**)
Carnival, 794, 926, 927-930, 1619
Causes fainting, 1633
Chalice of, 1208
Chance to show love, 303
Chosen souls sustain the world, 926
Closeness to God, 109
Come to a peak, 131
Comfort only in Jesus, 1461
Complaint to Jesus, 1161
Complete abandonment, 98
Confessor is fearful, 212

Confessors not understanding, 111

Confessor suffering from work on mercy, 86, 90

Confessor's role, 111

Conformed to Jesus in, 1697

Consent to, 136, 309, 488, 1032

Constant, 227

Constant companion, 316

Continuous physical suffering, 1633, 1636, 1637

Cost of sacrifice, 243

Coughing, 1085

Counsel of Father Andrasz, 506

Daily food, 276

Daily struggle, 1310

Dark night of the soul, 94-146

Darkness and temptations, 77

Darkness during novitiate, 23-27 (see also **Dark Night of The Soul**)

Darkness not understood by confessor, 211

Darkness of illusion, 211

Darkness of soul, 98, 1496, 1558, 1559

Decay of death, 1435

Decision to leave or not, 1263

Delight in heaven over a tested soul, 114

Denied by sister infirmarian, 1634

Desire for the truth, 131

Desire to, 853

Desire to drink the cup, 1484

Desire to resemble Christ, 1418

Desolation resolved by mercy, 1108

Deteriorated health, 1088

Difficulties overcome by Jesus, 788

Difficulty of suffering joyfully, 1152

Does not disturb inner silence, 1022

Does not know how to describe, 1656

Draining the cup, 697

Dreadful without Jesus crucified, 1508

Drinking the cup of bitterness, 1655

Drown in the Divine Heart, 792

Drown in the Merciful Heart of Jesus, 1550

During carnival, 1619

During Mass, 1657

During novitiate, 26

Effort needed to carry out duties, 1314

Embraced each day at Mass, 385

Emotions attack the intellect and will, 1152

Ending with help of two priests, 141

Ending year of, 1451

Ends with death, 1597

Entering school of, 1626

Envy of angels, 1804

Eucharist the strength to, 1509

Exhaustion, 496

Experience of abandonment, 109

Experience of despair, 771

Experience of Passion of Christ, 348, 349, 646, 672, 705, 759, 808, 913, 931, 964, 976, 996, 1010, 1016, 1028, 1034, 1035, 1053, 1054, 1055, 1060, 1079, 1196, 1274, 1276, 1277, 1305, 1468, 1515, 1536, 1627, 1646, 1663, 1724

Experience of thorn of Christ, 291, 1399, 1425 (see also **Passion**)

Experiencing inner suffering of, 694

Extreme physical pain, 1454, 1613

Eyes fixed on Jesus' Passion, 450

Faith struggles, 97

Fear of not pleasing God, 68

Fear of persons accosting, 1704

Feel complete decay, 1428

Fever, consuming no water!, 1647

First sign of sickness, 694

Five wounds, 1055

Fix eyes on Jesus, 1040

For Father Sopocko, 596

For Mardi Gras, 926, 927, 794

For mercy, for souls, 1647

For priest, 596

For priests, 41, 531, 596, 647, 823, 953, 988, 1212, 1607

For sinners, 893, 908, 926, 927, 999, 1428, 1640, 1645, 1743

For sinners and priests, 953

For soul in purgatory, 1186

For souls, 641, 842, 994, 1010, 1062, 1263, 1398, 1439, 1622

For triple crown, 604

Foreseeing the extent of, 22

Foretold, 22

Foretold by Blessed Virgin Mary, 25

Fortified for, 1067

Free consent, power in free act, 190

Freely with Jesus, 1454

Friends abandon and reproach like Job, 1509

From a person who lies, 1694

From accusations, 123, 200

From anxiety about the sanatorium, 1674

From causing others to suffer, 1349

From darkness of soul, yet faithful, 1235

From delaying on God's word, 715

From doubts and discouragement, 1488

From fearful confessor, 653

From food, 1428, 1554, 1633

From glory stolen from God, 1149

From grace of Eucharist wasted, 914

From heat, 701

From hideousness of sin, 1016

From humiliations of superiors, 128

From hypocrisy, 1579

From illusions, 122

From inadequacy, 68

From lies, 1150

From malice of a sister, 1492

From minor error, 1293

From misunderstanding, 1638

From neglect in the infirmary, 149, 1587, 1649

From news by a sister, 875

From Mother Superior's upbraiding, 133

From noise in the sanatorium, 804

From offence in the convent, 1144

From Passion, 948, 1016, 1060 (see also **Suffering: Experience of, Passion, Stigmata**)

From physical sickness, 1428, 1429, 1430

From presence of a cunning sister, 1494

From presence of others talking, 1476

From questions of sisters, 1236, 1555

From rash judgment of lay sis-

ters, 1716

From religious with self love, 1139

From remarks of the sisters, 1431

From rumors, 1150

From sisters, 125, 166, 168, 421, 632, 695, 710, 875, 1236, 1241, 1268, 1274, 1431, 1453, 1476, 1492, 1494, 1510, 1522, 1527, 1555, 1568, 1571, 1587, 1633, 1634, 1636, 1637, 1647, 1649, 1651, 1672, 1694, 1712, 1716, 1727

From sisters during illness, 710

From spiritual darkness, 1235

From superior, 1648 (see also **Mother Superior/General**)

From the heat, 701

From the world, 284

From visitors, 920

From weakness, 1545

From work of mercy destroyed for a time, 378

From worldly conversations, 1788

Glorifying Christ in suffering, 1662

Glorify His mercy, 697

God at work, 110

God comes to rescue, 1511

God's support moves us forward, 1606

God's will, 972

God's will and submitting to, 724

God's will be done, 1202, 1237

Grace of, 57

Graces after, 121

Graces supplied, 1341

Grave sickness in the sanitorium, 1679

Great grace, 57

Great pain of Passion, 1054

Great suffering of Redemption, 1643

Greater suffering the more like Jesus, 1394

Greatest from tension between obedience and inspiration, 1116

Greatest treasure, 342

Growth in virtue, 166

Harmonious melody, 385

Health is fading, 1729

Heart ached over grumbling sisters, 690

Heart sensitive to others, 692

Heart wounded by love, 943

Heavenly union on earth, 604

Heroic patience toward those who lay snares, 1241

Hiding in Merciful Heart of Jesus, 957

How a suffering soul is loved, 963

Humiliated by sister, 151

Humility after, 115

Hymns during, 114, 995, 1479, 1662

If the soul knew all at once it would die, 1655

Illness for advanced, 710

Impossible to live without the cross, 1112

In peace with God within, 455

In silence, 70, 126, 487, 667

In spreading devotion by Father Sopocko (?), 962

In trial, 100

In union with Jesus, for souls, 740

In work to be done, 1402

Infinite value joined to Jesus' suffering, 1512

Infirmarian neglects sister for a week, 1634, 1647

Ingratitude that flooded Jesus, 1538

Inner torment awakens trust, 672

Inner wounds of Christ, 705 (see above: **Experience of Passion of Christ**)

Intense mortification for a girl in trouble, 1305

Intensified suffering during carnival, 1619

Interior agony, 672

Interior stigmata, 759, 1055 (see also **Stigmata**)

Interior suffering advances in perfection, 981

Interior suffering over New Congregation, 644

Internal abandonment over New Congregation, 496

Ironic smiles, 662

Jesus always faithful, 1508

Jesus changes weakness into power, 1655

Jesus: conference on sacrifice and suffering, 1767

Jesus, do not leave me alone, 1489

Jesus, give me strength in drinking the cup, 1740

Jesus: you are a living host, 1826

Jesus: you will rejoice in heaven, 1787

Joy in, 303

Judged by sisters, 128

Judgments causing, 128, 133, 151, 165, 181, 236

Just a few more drops in the chalice, 694

Knowledge of self, 95

Known only to Jesus, 1633

Lack of understanding, 1113

Learn and go to Jesus, 1487

Leaves end of Mass, 1443

Lifted by appearance of Jesus, 103

Little sacrifices, 208

Looking to Jesus in silence, 1040

Loss of God's presence, 96

Loss of strength, 100

Love and, 1103

Love and sorrow go hand in hand, 843, 881

Love in the midst of, 1239

Love makes a delight, 303

Love of, 276, 278

Love united to, 1050

Love's quintessence, 1103

Makes for humility, 115

Makes for sensitivity to grace, 115

Makes for union with God, 115

Measure of love, 774

Meditation on the Passion, 267

Meditation on the Passion lessens suffering, 1626 (see also **Passion: Meditation on**)

Midnight Mass, 1441

Misinterpreted by sisters, 38

More severe than ever before, 653

Mortal sickness, 321

Mother Superior: you need to get used to suffering, 700

Must run its full course, 897

My name is "sacrifice," 135, 485

Mystery of, 110, 1656

Near death, 102, 999, 1786

Need of, 1612, 1762

Neglect of infirmarian, 149, 1587, 1647, 1649

New congregation anxieties, 496

No sacrifice for souls is insignificant, 971

No visitors, 827

Not able to attend Mass, 1453

Not alone, 1445

Not fearing, 106

Not wasted a minute, 1062

Not written about all of them, 1511

Nourished by God's will, 195

Obedience in, 102, 105

Obstacle to New Congregation, 662

Of being deserted, 746

Of body and visitation of the Lord, 1633

Of darkness Jesus, too, endured, 1487

Of death, 321, 323

Of decaying corpse known by Jesus, 1430

Of Father Sopocko, 1259

Of Father Sopocko rewarded in heaven, 596

Of Mother Superior, 1380

Of monotony and reluctance, 508

Of New Year's Day — sorrow and bitterness, 1453

Of Passion, 705 (see also **Suffering: Experience of, Passion, Stigmata**)

Of priest because of opposition, 1272

Of priests over work of mercy, 838

Of soul, 1116

Of soul and body, 653

Of stigmata (see **Stigmata**)

Offer patience when sister coughs continually, 1311

Offered, an abhorrence to Satan, 1464

Offered as sacrifice of love, 1316

Offered for sinners, 349

Offered weakness, 782

Offering in Eucharist, 385

Offering in silence, 831

Offering little sufferings, 1311

Offering of, 184, 190, 208, 1451

Offering self as a victim, 135, 308, 309, 1264, 1622, 1680

Offering self to please God, 1125

Offering self with Jesus for the world, 648

Offering temptation of student, 192

On Calvary with Christ, 1580

On earth, 36, 856

On moving to a new house, 1198-1202

On return from Rabka, 1236

On return to Cracow, 1207

Opposition and suffering in works of God, 270

Others' burdens carried, 1039

Over admonition by the confessor, 645

Over leaving the community, 655, 656

Over New Congregation, 644, 786, 1117, 1263

Over painting of the Image, 152

Over promotion of Divine Mercy Feast and Image, 74

Over warning of confessor, 74

Overall experience and comments, 22, 23, 24, 26, 27, 38, 57, 68, 70, 73, 77, 86, 90, 91, 92, 95, 97, 98, 100, 101, 102, 104, 106, 109, 114, 115, 116, 117, 119, 126, 128, 130, 133, 149, 151, 152, 165, 166, 181, 182, 184, 191, 196, 200, 208, 209, 211, 217, 227, 236, 253, 267, 268, 270, 276

Overcome by obedience, 1378

Pain from eating, 1554

Pain of death, 999
Pain of stigmata, 942, 1536 (see also **Stigmata**)
Pains of abortion, 1276
Passion of Christ (see above: **Suffering,** experience of, **Passion, Stigmata**)
Patience, 253
Pay no heed to, 1360
Peace does not leave, 1394
Peace in interior desolation, 1315
Peaceful behavior in, 1467
Peak, of during probation, 131
Persecutions, 91
Physical and moral, 1454
Physical condition beyond medical treatment, 1634
Physical effects of, 104
Physical weakness, 100
Pleasing God, 278
Prayer for strength in, 1065
Prayer in darkness, 73
Prayer of acceptance and glorifying, 1662
Prayer of *Te Deum* or *Magnificat*, 68
Prayer not always heard, 1656
Praying for those who make you suffer, 1628
Prediction of death, 1449
Preparing to receive Eucharist, 717
Priest suffering from ingratitude, 1547
Protracted sufferings accepted as gifts, 1795
Purification by, 38
Purifying, 109
Redoubling prayer, 1025
Reflections on, 208, 209, 253, 351, 831, 896, 1071, 1208, 1268
Refuge in Blessed Sacrament, 73

Relieved by Novena to Saint Therese, 150
Relying on God alone, 209
Renewed, 1464
Reproach of Mother Superior over sickness, 1648
Reproved by infirmarian, 1453
Request to share in the Passion, 1034 (see: **Suffering: Experience of Passion**)
Resignation to God's will, 696
Returns after a month of health, 1125
Run to the Heart of Jesus, 1033
Sacrifice flows from love, 784
Sacrifice makes soul useful, 1358
Sanitorium at Pradnik, 794, 798, 842
Satan stirs up discouragement, 129
Saves souls, 735, 1032
See Christ crucified in, 1268
Seeing God in trials, 227
Seek relief in prayer, 792

Seeking no comfort, 209
Sent to Pradnik, 794
Severe cough, 1088
Severe sickness, 1201
Share in suffering of Jesus because of love, 1487
Sharing the Passion in reparation for abortions, 1276, 1277
Sick, source of mercy, 1269
Sickness in infirmary, 149
Sickness near death, 696
Sickness, profit for souls, 67
Sign of God's presence, 669
Silence during, 126, 504, 1040, 1656
Sing of it by silence, 1490
Sins of Mardi Gras, 794, 926-930, 1619

Sisters not helping the ill, 1453
Sorrow of Passion, 977 (see also
   Passion)
Soul discouraged by persecution,
   1487
Soul is closest to Merciful Heart,
   1487
Soul steeped in bitterness, 896
Souls closest to Jesus taste bit-
   terness, 1402
Spiritual agony because of
   Image, 152
Springing out of the ground, 138
Springtime, soul in torment,
   1120
Stigmata, 976, 1196, 1247, 1468
   (see also **Passion, Stigmata**)
Strange apprehension, 1025
Strange darkness invades at
   times, 1124
Strength from Sacred Heart, 224
Strength given for Easter proces-
   sion, 1668
Strengthened by Eucharist, 876,
   1431, 1620
Strengthened by the Lord, 1051
Struggle during adoration, 268
Struggle of sickness, 1310
Submission in darkness, 78 (see
   also **Dark Night of The Soul**)
Submitted to will of God, 489,
   1204
Sudden experience of darkness,
   1108
Sudden healing, 1088, 1089
Superior's advice, 700
Surest way, 1394
Sustained by Eucharist, 1620
Sustained by grace, 1071
Taste of Passion, 872 (see also
   Passion)
Tension of obedience and God's
   will revealed, 981

Terrifying suffering, 1558
Thanks for, 343, 743
Thanks for four months of treat-
   ment, 1066
Thanks for illness, 1062
Thanks for the pieces of the
   cross, 382
There is nothing that could
   lessen my sacrifice, 1785
Thermometer of, is love, 343,
   774
Thorn, 1399, 1425 (see also
   Passion, Stigmata)
Through the year, 1451
Throughout a lifetime, 1655

Time for mercy, 133
Time of purification, 771
To save sinners, 1645
To the limit, 1612
Tongue causes, 118-120
Tormented by temptations of
   blasphemies, 673
Trial, 97
Trial of trials, 98, 99 (see also
   Dark Night of The Soul)
Trials and obedience, 102
Trials of purification, 97
Trust in, 697 (see also **Trust**)
Trust in the midst of, 1192, 1452
Trust in torrents, 681
Ugly to seek relief from, 387
Unable to attend Mass, 1453
Under God's justice, 101
Under the power of God, 101
Undeserved, 289
United to the Lord, 1207
United with Jesus, 1625
United with Jesus crucified,
   1201
Until death, 1597
Upheld by the Lord, 1051
Value of, 963

Victim for a sinner, 685
Victim of love, 726
Victims sustain the world, 604
Violent pains near death, 1613
Vision of suffering as victim, 135
Visit to doctor with anxious sister, 1636
Warning to prepare for, 488
What is done out of love is not small, 1310
When death nor health are given, 1509
With Christ, 1061
With Christ in the garden, 646
With Christ, the Passion, 1609 (see also **Passion**)
With fire of love, 46 (see also **Fire/Flames of Love**)
With Jesus, 1032, 1033, 1034, 1425, 1468, 1508, 1509, 1510, 1511, 1515, 1538, 1625, 1626, 1697
With Jesus on Palm Sunday, 1657
With joy, 432
With joy is not easy, 1152
With love, 1609
With patience, 115
With trust, 101
Words of Jesus, 67, 279, 282, 308, 310, 324, 488, 961, 965, 1612
Words of Sister Faustina on suffering for others, 57, 135, 136, 190, 192, 194, 195, 202, 203, 235, 239, 243, 276, 309, 311, 384, 385, 419, 482, 483, 485, 487, 488, 604, 605, 606, 705, 726, 871, 926, 927, 943, 963, 981, 1010, 1016, 1022, 1062, 1263, 1264, 1574, 1619, 1680
Work of God not understood at the time of, 1331
Work of mercy beyond her strength, 786
Wounded heart, 511
Writing in agony for sinners, 1451

Thanksgiving (for)

(see also **Glorifying Mercy**)
Advice of spiritual director, 1368
All God sends, 1549
Behalf of the ungracious, 719
Being a child of God, 1819
Being porter, 1313
Blessings of protection, 1489
Compels giving new graces, 1701
Confessor, 61
Continued all day, 1416
Conviction of reaching sanctity, 1333, 1361, 1362, 1410
Day of, 1661
Desire to live a life of, 1285
Eucharist greatest gift, 1670
Even for smallest of graces, 1701
Everything sent by God, 1208, 1549
Forgiveness, 1489
Gift of innocence, 1095
God for revealing faults, 900
God's mercy, 857
Graces and sacraments, 1286
Graces of the community, 1291
Graces received, 855, 1279, 1318, 1342, 1675, 1794
Great act of, 1367-1369
Hymn of, 1286, 1750 (see also **Hymns**)
Ingratitude pains Jesus, 698
Knowledge of misery, 256
Like a fire, 1368 (see also

Lord)
for His creatures to, 718, 1059
desire to encourage, 1234
to grant inconceivable graces to souls who, 687

Distrust hurts Jesus, 731

Distrust of a sister, 731

Distrust tears insides, 50

Distrust wounds, 1074

Dying soul filled with, after Chaplet, 1798

Encourage souls to, 1690

Entrust self, do not defend, 1727

Even if the ground gives way, 1192

Exhort souls to, 1567

Exhort to task of this life and next, 1637

Exhortation to anxious sister, 1637

Faith is necessary for Christ to act, 1420

Faustina to urge all souls to, 294, 1059, 1182

Faustina's "mission" to convince people to, 1452 (see also **Mission)**

Fear nothing, 589

Fills to abundance of graces, 1074

For grace of union, 91 (see also **Union)**

Forces graces, 718

God cares, 922

Grace of absolute confidence in mercy, 1337

Great trust even with crushed heart, 1552

Greatest Glory, 930

Greatest sinners have the greatest right to, 723, 1146

Grows stronger with self-knowledge, 1406

Guarantee of peaceful death, by, 1520
by encouraging others to, 1540

Have confidence in God, 880

Hope advances to, 386

Hurt by distrust, 300

Hymn, 2, 4, 1298, 1322, 1748

"If only" souls would trust, they sould achieve great sanctity, 1784

Image and words, "Jesus, I trust in You," as vessel for grace, 327

Immerse self in mercy with, 1361 (see also **Baptism in His Mercy**

In difficult moments, 944

In Divine Mercy gives greatest glory, 930 (see also **Glorifying Mercy)**

In Him who can do all, 358

In Jesus, 249

In Merciful Heart of Jesus, 1138 (see also **Merciful Heart of Jesus**

In mercy of God, 69, 615, 687, 854, 898, 992, 1064, 1065, 1118, 1195, 1325, 1452, 1639, 1730

In sacrifice, 908

In spite of feelings, 24

In the power of grace, 1371

In the power of mercy, 1479

In the Holy Trinity, 357

Inciting to, 1582

Jesus and lack of, 50, 300, 379, 1076, 1447

Jesus desires great trust in His mercy, 1059

Jesus, I trust in You, 162, 239, 327, 859, 860, 1209

Jesus refers to souls, calls them most fortunate,

1273

delights to work in them, 1784

gives them priority to His mercy, 1541

loves them, 294, 453, 1541

promises all things to them, 294, 453

Jesus wounded by lack of, 1486

Joy to Jesus, 1578

Justification of soul dependent on, 570

Lack of, in chosen souls, 731

Lesson in total, 1559

Let sinners trust in mercy, 1146

Like a child, 1541

Measure of generosity dependent on, 548, 1602

Mercy received by souls who, 420

Mercy will always embrace a soul who, 1777

Mistrust displeases, 595

Mistrust of many, 287

More I feel misery the stronger grew trust, 1817

More trust the more received, 1578

Most dear to the Lord, 453

Need of, 1577, 1777

Never in self, 1760

New Congregation for income, 548

Not disappointed, 1480

Not frustrated, 746

"O Blood and Water," 84, 187, 309

Obtain for the dying, 1777

Obtainable through Sister Faustina, 1777

Omnipotence of, 1777

One vessel of mercy, 1578

Only source of peace, 300

Opens door to immensity of graces, 1074

Peace at death, 1520

Peaceful death guaranteed by, 1520, 1798

Place all in Lord, 317

Placed complete trust in mercy, 1679

Placed in God, 681

Power of soul, 198

Prayer of, 84, 187

Requisite for advancing in perfection, 1578

Requisite for peace for mankind, 300

Restrains God's justice, 198

Rewards of,
  salvation, 723
  sanctity, 1784

Soul filled with, after words of Mary, 677

Soul that trusts is most fortunate, 1273

Souls and, 1577, 1578

Source of graces, 1577, 1777

Take vessel of, and draw on mercy, 1488

Tell souls to, 294

Transformed into, 1489 (see also **Transformation**)

Urge all to, 1182

Vessel for obtaining graces, 1485, 1578

Vessel to draw mercy in confession, 1602

Victory on enemies, 723

While in misery, 69

Union
(see also **Desires of Sister Faustina, Fire/Flames of Love, Heart, Love, Holy Trinity, Presence of God, Spiritual Life,**

Transformation)

Absorbed in God, 913
Advice of confessor needed, 773
All afire, 142
All else is fleeting, 1141
At Mass, 471
Aware of Christ's presence, 560
Because of humility and love, 587
Bethany for Jesus, 735
Beyond language, 767
By an act of the will in suffering, 1207
By cooperating with grace, 204
Call at age of seven, 7
Call to constant, 576
Call to espousal, 912
Close intimacy, 629
Close with Jesus, 1109
Closer than other creatures, 1546
Commune with God in depths of own being, 1302
Communing with Jesus, 603
Condescending love, 854
Constantly, 971
Continually, 1544
Degrees of glory, 605
Depends on our cooperation, 771
Desire for, 761
Desire for greatest intimacy, 1631
Desire of Jesus, 1542
Desire to be eternally in, 1303
Drawn into the Father's Heart, 1279
Drowned in God, 771
Drowned in Him, 729, 1500, 1523
Embraced by greatness of God, 1780
Enveloped and transpierced, 983
Exclusive Communion with Bridegroom, 1021
Exclusive intimacy with Jesus, 1693
Gift of God, 480, 771
God's action, 767
Grace granted by mercy, 1576
Grace of union received, 771
Grace to suffer, 772
Granted grace of union, 1057
Great mystery accomplished, 138
Heart to Heart, 1056
Immersed in God in presence of a priest, 891
In heaven, 107
In life and death, 1552
In suffering, 784
Intense presence prolonged, 411
Interior espousal, 1020
Intimate communion, 622
Inundated with love, 997
Jesus calls to a unique intimacy, 707
Jesus delights in, 570, 954
Jesus is constant companion, 318
Jesus left heaven to be, 1810
Jesus makes it possible to commune with Him, 708
Jesus unites Himself to Sister Faustina, 824
Joy of presence, 491
Knowledge of in others, 769
Like a drop in ocean, 702
Lord's desire for, 826
Lost in God, 1416
Lost in God at Communion, 1807
Love alone explains, 885
More close than in mother's womb, 883
New Congregation to please God by, 572
Nothing disturbs, 803, 883, 1135

Of hearts, 239, 1021 (see also **Heart, Merciful Heart of Jesus**)

Of love with God, 1334

On glorifying the Father, 577

Only love understands, 729

Penetrated by God's light, 1681

Penetrates, 480

Pervading, 582

Possession of soul, 734

Prayer for, 832

Purely spiritual, 767

Received at age of 18, 770

Recognized in kindred souls, 768

Resolution to unite with the Heart of Jesus, 905

Response of humility, 771

Retreat resolution, 1105

Returns after dryness, 1246

Short, but effective, 767

Snuggling close to the Sacred Heart, 138

Some called to a higher, 1556

Soul drowned in, 989

Soul immersed in God, 137

Soul is divinized, 771

Soul is protected by, 1094

Source of lights, 733

Special series of teachings on, 767-785

Spiritual union at Communion, 1278

Sustained by a miracle of God, 767

Through love at Communion, 1815

Through suffering, 115, 604

Time passes quickly, 784

Transconsecrated, 137

Transformed into love, 142

Unceasingly with love, 1443

Unique mystery, 824

Unique with Jesus, 587

Wings set for flight, 142

With Christ taught by Blessed Virgin Mary, 786

With God, 346

With God be prepared for battles, 121

With God each free moment, 703

With God is perfection, 457

With Jesus, 467

With Jesus at Mass, 1262

With Jesus intimate, 603

With sacrifice of Christ, 482

With the Father, 626

With the Holy Trinity, 486, 507, 1073, 1129 (see also **Holy Trinity**)

With the Lord, 1169

Wth the Lord, purpose of life, 729

With the merciful Christ, 703, 742, 790. 1352 (**Merciful Heart of Jesus**)

With whole heart, 947

Word spoken from is precious, 1595

You are the delight of My Heart, 137

Urgency
(see **Judgment, Second Coming**)

Veil of Heaven
80, 281, 386, 483, 522, 524, 807, 930

Virtues
(see also **Gems of Sister Faustina, Grace, Humility, Love, Obedience, Religious Life, Silence, Spiritual Life, Vows**)

Against hope in God's mercy,

309

Faith maintains the soul, 210

Heroic virtue and sacrifice, 208

Jesus: bear everything patiently that befalls you, 1701

Joy return to Cracow for retreat, 216

Patience,
>great power in, 1514
>of God, with us children, 1524
>practice of, 179, 181, 182
>tested by visitor, 920

Peace,
>deepest yet, 1660
>gift of God, 143
>no peace until, 699
>nothing disturbs inner peace, 1134
>remain in, 219

Penance, glory be to the Father, 577

Practice, of, 179, 181

Prudence, defined, 1106

Prudence, part of all virtues, 1106

Purity,
>confirmed in, 1096
>constantly on the watch, 1098
>gift of, 40, 1095
>of intention, 66
>special mercy, 1099

Suffers, 236

Test of, by sisters, 196

Visions, Eucharist

(see also **Eucharist: Vision of**)

After Holy Communion, 826

As an infant/child and Our Lady, 25, 529, 677, 846, 1585

As in Image at Communion, 613

At Communion, 498, 1816

At Eucharist, adoration, 433, 691

At Eucharist, scourged, 614

At Mass, 512, 1053

At Mass, Jesus suffering, 1512, 1663

At Mass as a child/infant, 312, 345, 406, 434, 442, 575, 659, 879, 1346, 1820

At the Last Supper, 684, 757

Ciborium filled with Hosts, 709

During Benediction, 464

During Holy Hour, suffering, 1599

During Resurrection Mass, 1067

Eucharist, 597

Face of Jesus in the Eucharist, 1420

Host, 616

In great beauty at Mass, 438

In the cenacle at the instituting of Eucharist, 684, 757

In the Host, 44, 160, 406, 413, 433

In the Host with rays, 991, 1046

Without vestments, 991

Visions, General

Angel, 20, 471

Angel above each church, 630

Angel at the gate, 1271

Angel bringing Holy Communion, 1676

Angel of wrath, Trinity, words of Chaplet, 474

Beyond senses of knowledge of God and self, 882

Blessed Virgin Mother, 805 (see also **Mary, Mother of God: Visions of Our Lady**)

Blessed Virgin Mary, breast bared and pierced pierced with a sword, 686

Book of life, 689
Cenacle, 684
Chastisement of a city, 39
Child Jesus, on love and humili-
ty, 424-427
Child pointing to the moon and
stars, 424
Children in need of defense from
evil, 765
Ciborium, 285, 709
Clergy at the altar, 31
Confessor, 53
Confessor celebrating Mass, 447
Convent of the New
Congregation, 559, 563, 765,
892, 1154
Cross and Jesus in light, 603
Cross over world, 34
Crystal dwelling with three
doors, 420
Destruction of convents and
churches, 1702
Eucharist, souls converted by
prayer and suffering, 709
Father Sopocko, 61, 1547
Father Sopocko working at desk,
762
Feast celebrated by Pope in
Rome and Cracow, 1044
God, at age seven, 7
God gazing into her heart, 1025
Guardian angel, 419, 470, 490
Guardian angel and her throne in
heaven, 683
Hard times, Mass in homes, 991
Heaven, 777, 778, 779, 1604,
1681
Heaven of saints and Sister
Faustina, 683
Heavenly throne, 85
Hell, 43, 741
Holy Trinity, 30
Living Hosts, 640
Mary (see **Mary, Mother of**

God)
New Congregation, convent, 765
(see also **New Congregation**)
Ostra Brama of Jesus and Mary,
529
Palace, 1563
Pillars, 1689
Pope, 1080
Pope in Rome celebrating the
Feast, 1044
Pope Pius XI, 368
Purgatory, 20, 58, 412, 424, 425,
426
Purgatory and Our Lady, 20
Questioned as illusions, 54
Rays from the Host, 657 (see
also **Eucharist: Rays from,
Rays**)
Roads to hell and heaven, 153
Roses, 65
Saint Barbara, asking for Holy
Communion for Poland, 1251
(see also **Saints**)
Saint Ignatius and the rule, 448
Saint Joseph, 607, 608, 846,
1442
Saint Michael, 706
Saint Therese, 150
Saints at the throne interceding
for Poland, 689
Saints of Jesuits in heaven, 683
Satan in guise of guardian angel,
1405
Soul being judged, 425
Soul crucified like Christ, 446
Soul in purgatory, 594
Souls in torment, 426
Souls from purgatory, 21
Spiritual director in, 378
Struggle of light and dark, 307
Three souls leaving purgatory,
748
Two pillars supporting a temple,
1689

Visions of Jesus

Above the chapel, 87

After a dry prayer, 691

After a time of spiritual warfare, 1499

After confession, 894

After Holy Communion, 826

After serving the sick, 1029

And Our Lady, 88, 330, 529, 561, 608, 677, 846, 1261, 1442, 1710

As a child, 335, 347, 427

As an infant/child and Our Lady, 25, 529, 677, 846, 1585

As an infant during Communion, 566

As an infant Jesus in the chalice, 1820

As father confessor, 817

As in Image adorned with lamps, 851

As in Image with confessor and spiritual director writing, 675

As in the Image, 473, 560, 613, 645, 1047

As in the Image and Our Lady, 561

As in the Image blessing, 420

As in the Image under a mesh, 416

As in the Image with rays from His Heart, 1565

As the Eucharist, 1053

At Communion, 498, 1816

At Eucharist, adoration, 433, 691

At Eucharist, scourged, 614

At her *prie dieu*, 489

At Mass, 1053

At Mass as a child/infant, 312, 345, 347, 406, 434, 442, 562, 575, 609, 659, 879, 1346, 1820

At sanatorium, 799

At shore of lake, 158

At the Last Supper, 684

At Vespers, 858

Blessing Sister Faustina, 54

Blessing the people on the Feast, 1048

Call to suffering, 36

Clasping Sister Faustina to His Heart, 928, 929

Consoling with peace, 674

Cross and light, 603

Crucified, 446, 669, 913, 988

Crucified with jewels pouring from His wounds, 1687

Crucifix comes alive, 669

During a conference, 464

During Benediction, 151

During confession, 466

During Holy Hour, suffering, 1599

During Resurrection Mass, 1067

Dying, 976

Entering one of three doors, 420

Eucharist, 597

Eucharist, Mass, 512, 1053

Exposed Monstrance, 1420

Expressing His love for Sister Faustina, 853

Father looking at Jesus Crucified, 60

Father looks at earth through the wounds of Jesus, 60

Gift of purity, 40

Holy Trinity, 30 (see also **Holy Trinity**)

In all majesty with Mary interceding, 1261 (see also **Mary, Mother of God**)

In beauty, 853

In Easter glory, 1669

In great beauty, 980, 1069

In great beauty at Mass, 438

In her cell, 776

In great majesty, 587, 881, 1246

In His Passion past and present, 445-446

In His Passion praying, 736

In His Passion tortured, 948

In Passion, 19, 36, 252, 408, 583, 639, 648, 736, 737, 948, 964 (see also **Passion**)

In radiant garb, 415

In sorrow, 19

In tears, 286

In the Cenacle at the instituting of Eucharist, 684, 757

In the Host, 44, 160, 406, 413

In the Host with rays, 1046 (see also **Eucharist, Rays**)

In the Image, 417

In the kitchen, 28

In white robe and rays of red and pale, 47

Jesus on the Feast of Mercy, 1044-1048

King, with severity, 1261

Lamb of God, 689

Looking into her soul, 858

Nativity, 1442

Offended by children, 765

On Good Friday (1936), three o'clock, 648

On Palm Sunday, 642

On the cross, 1032, 1184

On the cross looking at the sisters, 383

On the cross with rays as in Image, 648

Passion, 583 (see also **Passion**)

Pearls and diamonds from His Heart, 1687

Piercing gaze, 324

Radiant as the sun, 415

Radiant, Crucified Christ, 60

Radiant wounds, 30, 205

Rays from His Heart, 87, 414, 1559, 1796 (see also **Rays**)

Resurrected, 205

Reviewing her note book, 459

Scourged, 188, 445, 526, 614, 639, 737

Sister Faustina holds Baby Jesus, 1442

Sudden apparition of Jesus, 1069

Suffering Lord, 1645

Taking her heart with Him, 42

Throne of the Lamb with Polish saints, 689

Tortured, 9, 1666

Watching Sister Faustina, 1693

With clergy, 344

With Father Andrasz, 712

With Sister Faustina at the altar, 1048

With sword and balance, 394

Your love is pure, 1061

Visit Home

Dying mother, 396

Father's prayer, 398

Joy of visit, 397

Parish church, 400

Visitors, 401, 402, 403

Vocation

Acceptance to religious life, 14

Age seven, 7

August 1925, enters convent, 17

Call of God, 8

Dance, 9

Longing for God, 15

Mass, words of Jesus, "Go to that priest," 12

Prayer, Mary lead me ..., 11

Priest, have confidence, 13

Temptation to leave, 18

Vision of Jesus, "Go at once to Warsaw," 10

Vow of chastity, 16

Work period, 15

Vows
(see also **New Congregation, Obedience, Religious Life, Spiritual Life, Virtues**)
Anticipation of, 238
Catechism of, 93
Chastity at age of 18, 771
Chastity has power, 534
Chastity, vow and virtue, 93
Day of final vows, 239
Final reflection upon, 254
Final vows joined to Passion, 250
Meditation on life of Jesus, 533
Perpetual, 199
Poverty, vow and virtue, 93
Reflection on final vows, 231
Renewal of, 468
Vision of the sword of the Lord outweighed, 394
Words of Bishop, 248

Words of Angels
(see also **Angels**)
Singing, 1111
Singing Sister Faustina's life history, 1202

Words of God
(see also **Words of Jesus**)
Mercy passing through the Heart of Jesus, 528
On mercy and justice and purgatory, 20
"You are My well-beloved daughter," 1681

Words of Jesus
Abyss filled with mercy, 1576
Accept all sufferings with love, 1767
Accept with gratitude everything given, 1381

Accompany Me to the sick, 183
Act like a beggar and ask, 294
Acting with purity of intention, 1566
Action on your own does not please Me, 659
Adoration for mercy, 1070
All comes from the depths of mercy, 699
All is in bowels of mercy, 1076
All My works are exposed to great suffering, 1643
All need mercy, 1577
All that exists is yours, 969
All this (at the lake) I created for you, 158
Allow nothing to disturb your peace, 1685
Always be merciful, 1446
Angels have profound knowledge, 1332
Any desire? It will happen soon (united forever), 1700
Any difficulties in this retreat? 1772
Apostle of My mercy, proclaim My mercy, 1142
Approach Eucharist with trust, 1487
Archbishop's response, 586
Ardor of heart is pleasing to, 826
Are not My visits every day enough? 827
As judge, sign of cross in sky, 83
As you are united in life, so united in death, 1552
As you ask so shall it be, 609
Ask for graces, 294
Ask mother to wear a hair shirt, 28
Ask my faithful servant to preach mercy on the Feast,

Asking for a holocaust of the will, 923

Assurance of income for New Congregation, 548

At Communion desires union, 1385

At Easter procession, be filled with joy, 1669

At Mass, "Look into My Heart," 1663

At the Mass offered by Father Sopocko, 1408

At three o'clock,
    any difficulties with this retreat? 1772
    immerse self in mercy, 1572
    implore mercy for sinners, this is the hour of great mercy, 1320
    try to make the stations or visit the Blessed Sacrament, 1572
    you can obtain everything, 1572

Be a victim of love, 726

Be at peace, I am with you, 133, 143, 145, 215, 219, 757, 799, 1676

Be comforted that souls will be saved, 966

Be filled with joy, 415

Be filled with mercy, 167

Be frank with your confessor, 1499

Be grateful for the smallest graces, teaching on interior life, 1701

Be like a knight in battle, 1823

Be little toward your confessor, 1260

Be merciful as I am, 1695

Be merciful to others, come to the fount of mercy, 1486

Be obedient to spiritual director, his word is My will, 979

Be obedient to your confessor, 1374

Be open to my representative, 494, 968, 1725

Be patient, others will tell her (negligent nurse), 1587

Be silent when truth is not acknowledged, 1164

Be watchful, lose no opportunity for sanctification, 1361

Bear patiently all that befalls you, 1701

Beg for mercy for the whole world, 570

Behold the treasures that flow from my heart, 1687

Being a pliant tool, 1359

Being a saint, 1571

Blessing of the neighborhood, 719

Boundless sincerity with the spiritual director, 1561

Boundless trust in mercy, 1578

Bride is to resemble the bridegroom, 268

Bring your ear close to My Heart, 229

By striving for perfection you will sanctify many, 1165

By the Image I shall grant many graces, 570

By this Novena (of Chaplets) I will grant every possible grace, 796

By your entreaties you will obtain mercy, 435

Call on My mercy for sinners, 186

Call to be victim, 135, 136, 137, 138

Call to faith, 352, 353

Calling to her vocation, 9

Cancel out your will, 372

Care for two pearls, priests and religious, 531

Cares even for the insects, 922

Chaplet brings mankind closer to Me, 929

Chastity, 534

Child, speak no more of your misery, 1485

Childlike spirit, 332

Children uphold the world, 286

Chosen souls illumine the world as stars at night, 1601

Chosen souls without love I cannot stand, 1702

Close to My Heart meditate on graces received, 1327

Closest union with Sister Faustina, 707

Come close to the source of mercy, glorify my mercy, 1485

Come to Me all of you, 1485

Communing with Sister Faustina, 603

Conference on mercy, 1777

Conference on sacrifice and prayer, 1767

Conference on spiritual warfare, 1760 (see also **Spiritual Warfare**)

Confessor, 1725 (see also **Confessor, Fathers**)

Confessor of Sister Faustina, 1163

Consider: and being in agony, He prayed more earnestly, 157

Consider: I loved you before I made the world, 1754

Consider: life of God in the Church, 1758

Consider: love of neighbor, 1768

Consider: My love in the Eucharist, I am entirely yours, 1770

Consider: My sufferings before Pilate, 149

Consider: the Passion, 1761

Consider: the rule and vows, 1763

Consider: the religious life as a source of grace, 1763

Contemplating His attributes, 30

Continuing with effort the work of mercy, 1374

Converse with Me in your heart, 581

Created beauty, 158

Creates out of mercy, 85

Cross at Eucharist, 1628

Daily martyrdom saves souls, 1184

Daily visits, 827

Darkness of the soul, 1559

Deeds of mercy, 742, 1267

Delight in coming in Communion to religious souls, 1683

Delight in her heart, 339

Delight in her love, 1546

Delight of My Heart, 1193

Delighting the Trinity, 955

Dependence, 659

Desire and theme for a New Congregation, 438

Desire to be a saint, 1361

Desires a New Congregation, 437

Devote all your free time to writing, 1693 (see also **Write/Writing**)

Difficulties prove that the work is Mine, 1295

Dispense My mercy, relieve My sorrow, 975

Distressed souls have a priority to mercy, 1541

Distribute graces as you will, 31

Distrust, 50, 1532

Distrust wounds Me, 580, 1076

Distrust wounds My Heart, 628

Do all for souls, 1184

Do all you can for the work of mercy, 998 (see also **Work of Mercy**)

Do as much work as obedience allows, 1644

Do not be absorbed in misery, 1486

Do not be afraid, 1180

Do not be afraid of suffering, 151

Do not be afraid of the Father's house, 290

Do not be afraid of what will happen, 1491

Do not be discouraged by difficulties, 1142

Do not be guided by feeling but by the will, 1760

Do not be sad, tell the Archbishop what you saw, 473

Do not be surprised at accusations, 289

Do not cry, you accompanied Me in suffering and death, 1061

Do not exert yourself with words, 739

Do not fear, exhort souls to trust in My mercy, 1452

Do not fear ... you will remain here, 1180

Do not fear about New Congregation, 881

Do not fear because special graces are given, 1753

Do not fear, I am with you, 103, 258, 431, 435, 541, 613, 626, 627, 629, 634, 645, 675, 881, 1133, 1150, 1704

Do not fear, I am your strength, My mercy is greater than all sins, 1485

Do not fear suffering, 151

Do not omit Communion, 156

Do not pay attention to murmurs, 1464

Do not place obstacles to mercy, 1577

Do not put off the Sacrament of Penance, 1464

Do not rely on people but on Me, 1487

Do not speak about your opinions, 1492

Do not speak to a certain sister, 1492

Do not tie My hands (regarding Russia), 818

Do not tire proclaiming mercy, 1521

Do not weep, 259

Do not weep, I grant your prayer, 928, 929

Do not worry, man can do nothing of himself, 1610

Do not worry much about adversities, 1643

Do not yield to vain terror, 453

Do only what you receive permission to do, 560

Do the will of the superior, 329

Do what is within your power, 881

Do what obedience allows, 1650

Do what you can in the work of mercy, 1295

Do whatever you can to spread the devotion of My mercy, 1074

Doyou believe me now? (change in a ward), 74

Do you need anything? 1682

Do you want to act like that?
(run from the battle), 287

Doing the works of mercy, 1644

Draw on the abyss of My mercy
for self and sinners, 1777

During a Eucharistic procession:
here is My repose, 1136,
1140

During Eucharist: be obedient to
your spiritual director, 979

Eight day retreat, 1327 (see also
Retreat)

Encourage sinners to come to
My mercy, 1059

Encourage souls to trust, 294

Encourage the Chaplet, 1541

Enormous are the debts of the
world paid by sacrifice of
pure souls, 1316

Enter often into purgatory, they
need you, 1738

Entrust self to Me at death, 1543

Eternal Father, I offer You, 475

Eternal Life begins in
Communion, 1811

Eucharist, 1770 (see also
Eucharist: Words of Jesus)

Every movement of your heart is
known to Me, 588

Every time you enter the chapel
pray ... Eternal Father, 476

Everything in the bowels of
mercy, 1076

Everything you say about My
goodness is true, 359

Faith in the Eucharistic presence, 1420, 1421, 1422

Faith is necessary for Me to act,
1420

Faithful souls who love, 1703

Fall of the angels, 1332

Father, 290

Father Andrasz will lead you, do
not fear 712 (see also **Father
Andrasz**)

Father Sopocko, 53, 86, 263,
1256, 1408 (see also **Father
Sopocko**)

Faults against your director
wound Me, 362

Fear not, 103, 129, 797, 1704

Fear not, I will not leave you
alone, 258, 573, 630, 643, 655

Feast, 49, 206, 299, 300, 341,
570, 1517

Feast as a refuge, 699

Feast comes from the depths for
consolation, 1517

Feast, Confession and
Communion, 1109

Feast emerged from the depths
of My mercy, 420

Feast is the last hope of salvation, 965

Feeling His absence, 413

Feeling suffering for sinners,
1357

Few souls contemplate My
Passion, 737

Fight for souls, 1489

Fight like a knight (spiritual
warfare), 1760

Fix your eyes on My holy will,
1327

Flame of pity for sinners burns
Me, 1521

Flames of mercy are burning
Me, 1074, 1190

Flowers, 71

For the sake of His triple crown
(reason for Father Sopocko
suffering), 604

For your sake I am hastening the
Feast, 1082

For your sake I bless the earth,
980, 1061, 1078

For your sake I bless the entire
country, 39

From the heart of My beloved must spring My mercy, 1148

Gaze of the Image is gaze from the cross, 326

Gaze on My Merciful Heart, 1486

Generosity of Jesus, 1687

Get to know God by His attributes, 30

Gift of purity, 40

Give Me souls, 1690

Gives five directives on spiritual warfare, 1560

Gives more than Sister Faustina desires, 1169

Giving understanding to the Archbishop, 473

Glorify Me by fulfilling My desires, 500

Glorify My mercy by immersing all sinners, 206

Glory of obedience over mortifications, 894

Go and console him (Father Sopocko), 466

Go to that priest and tell him all, 12

Go to Warsaw; enter a convent, 10

Goodness of Jesus, 359

Grace of perpetual vows, 165

Grace of retreat, 167, 169

Grace of the Image, 313

Grace to rise above human scorn, 1164

Graces for meditating on the Passion, 738

Graces given because of love, 383

Graces misery and mercy, 723

Graces not accepted, 1017

Graces not given to others, are given daily, 1753

Graces promised for saying Chaplet, 848

Grape in a cluster, 393

Gratitude for praise, 1707

Great trust, 718

Greater the sinner the greater the mercy, 723

Greatest obstacles: discouragement and sensitivity are fruit of self-love, 1488

Greatest obstacles to holiness are discouragement and anxiety, 1488

Greatest sinners will achieve sanctity by trust in My mercy, 1784

Happy the soul that has immersed itself in the fountain of mercy, 1075

Hate of Satan, 412

Have boundless sincerity with spiritual director, a great grace, 1561

Have you exhausted the retreat subject? 1756

He [Father Sopocko] is after My Heart, 1256

He who refuses to pass through the door of mercy, 1146

He who trusts will not perish, all his enemies will be shattered, 723

He [Father Andrasz] will lead you, 712

Heart of Jesus as a fount of mercy, 1520

Heart of My Heart, 1669

Heart of the beloved must resemble Mine, 1148, (see also **Merciful Heart of Jesus**)

Help in the retreat, 213

Help Me save sinners, 1645

Help Me save souls by your suffering, 1032, 1797

Help Me save the soul of a dying man, 1797

Help needed to accept graces, 738

Here is My resting place, 1140

Hinderance to the work of mercy, 1295

His [Father Sopocko] heart is a heaven on earth, 574

His suffering for salvation of souls, 1184

Holy Trinity finds delight in you, 955

Hour of death, 1539

Hour of mercy, 1370

How amazed you will be to see Me in glory, 1810

How can they [religious] sit in judgment who are more guilty? 1702

How great is My joy at faithfulness, 352

How is your retreat? 295

How long will you put Me off, 9

How miserable are those who do not take advantage of the miracle of mercy, 1448

How much distrust hurts Me, 300

How to recite the Chaplet, 476

Human plans will be thwarted, 1180

Humble prayer disarms the anger of God, 320

Humility, 1293, 1361, 1563 (see also **Humility**)

I accept you, 14

I am a Merciful Savior to those who spread mercy, 1075

I am always in your heart, 575

I am always with you, 1011

I am coming first as King of Mercy, 83

I am delighted with your love, 1546

I am granting (your family) special graces, 401

I am happy to be at home in heart of Father Andrasz, 879

I am hastening the Feast, 1082

I am in your heart, 609

I am King of Mercy, 88

I am Love and Mercy, 1273

I am Mercy, 300

I am Mercy Itself ... offer Me your misery, 1775

I am Mercy Itself for the contrite, 1739

I am more merciful to sinners than the just, 1275

I am offering a vessel (Image) for mercy, 327

I am pained at Holy Communion without faith, 1288

I am pained by mistrust after a fall, 1532

I am pleased by Chaplet for humanity, 929

I am pleased by love, 1489

I am pleased by service of mercy, 1029

I am pleased to rest in your heart, 1136

I am pleased with your efforts, but why so sad? 1488

I am pleased with your response to Satan, 1499

I am pleased with your sharing with family, 404

I am preparing graces for you in this retreat, 167

I am sad because souls do not have My Spirit, 1478

I am saddened by souls who ask for little, 1378

I am searching for souls who receive My grace, 1705

I am sending a day of mercy

before justice, 1588

I am sending two sisters to visit, 1494

I am taking you into my school of suffering, 1626

I am taking your heart, 42

I am the Lord, 85

I am thrice Holy and I detest sin, 1728

I am uniting with you in a special way, 603

I am very much at home in his heart [Father Andrasz], 879

I am watching over you, 1494

I am your patron, 360, 362

I am your teacher, 1701

I appear as a child to teach spiritual childhood, 1481

I ask that the priest preach on mercy, 1072

I bear a special love for Poland, I will exalt her, a spark will come from her, 1732

I bestow special grace on souls you intercede for, 599

I bless the earth because of you, 1078

I bless those you plead for, 599

I bless you with joy, 1824

I bring difficulties and I overcome them, 788

I came from heaven for sinners, 1275

I came to taste the fruits of her mercy [to the beggar boy], 1312

I can do all things in a moment, 1153

I can do nothing with souls who judge and talk about others, with envy, 1717

I cannot bear ingratitude, 1537

I cannot exalt the proud community, 1170

I care for souls' sanctification if they turn to Me, 1682

I change work into perfume, 65

I claim veneration for My mercy from every creature, 1572

I come out to meet you, 1705

I commune with you because you do not hoard My gifts, 1069

I confirm in peace, 229

I deal with you as a perfect soul, 1359

I delight in those who trust, 1541

I delight in you as living host, 923

I demand a childlike spirit, 332

I demand a holocaust of will, 923

I demand deeds of mercy, 742

I demand obedience, 28

I demand worship of My mercy by the Feast and Image, 742

I demand you glorify My mercy, 742

I desire a congregation of mercy, 437 (see also **Desire / Demands of Our Lord**)

I desire great trust in My mercy, 1059

I desire My mercy to flow through you to the world, 1777

I desire offering of self, 308

I desire priests proclaim mercy to sinners, 50

I desire striving souls to have boundless trust, 1578

I desire the Feast to be a refuge for all, especially sinners, 699

I desire the Image be publicly honored, 414

I desire the Image to be displayed on the Feast of Mercy,

I desire to enter the heart of sinners, 1485

I desire to give unimaginable graces to those who trust, 687

I desire to heal mankind, 1588

I desire to pour mercy on all "if only" souls would trust, 1784

I desire to rest in your hands, 159

I desire transformation of you, 726

I desire union, 1542

I desire union with souls in Holy Communion, 1385

I desire you accompany Me, 183

I desire you burn as a pure victim of love, 726

I desire your heart to be in peace, 459

I died and created the heavens for you, 853

I don't demand mortification but obedience, 28

I dwell in the tabernacle as King of Mercy, 367

I dwell in your heart as in a chalice, 1346, 1820

I enter some souls unwillingly at Communion, 1598, 1658

I excluded no one from the fount of mercy opened on the cross, 1182

I expect many to glorify My mercy, 1489

I find no rest in talkative souls, 1008

I give everything in a moment, 1153

I give more than you desire, 1169

I give nothing beyond his strength, 1607

I give you a portion of My Passion, 1053

I give you eternal love (gift of purity), 40

I give you graces to witness to mercy, 400

I give you profound peace (as a sign), 143

I give you the exclusive privilege of drinking the cup, 1626

I give you the first place among the virgins, 282

I give you three ways of exercising mercy, 742

I grant the grace because of complete obedience to your director, 365

I grant the sisters many graces because of your love, 383

I grant you the grace of union out of mercy, 1576

I have a place for him [Father Andrasz], 967

I have come to meet you, 1705

I have given up on souls who thwart My efforts, 1682

I have given you a profound understanding of My mercy, 1572

I have given you the opportunity for deeds of mercy, 1267

I have prepared the sanatorium for you, 1674

I keep company with you as a child to teach humility, 184

I know I know all things, 427

I know My will is dearer to you than life, 707

I know what you can do; I will give orders but delay their being carried out, 923

I know your efforts rest close to My Heart, 902

I leave souls quickly if anyone else is present, 1683

I left My throne to be with you in Communion, 1810

I made him known to you [Father Sopocko], 268

I Myself am your director, 362

I need sacrifice of love, 1316

I need suffering to save souls, 1612

I offer complete remission on the Feast, 1109

I offer a share in redemption, 310

I often wait with great grace until the end of prayer, 268

I overcome difficulties, 788

I prolong time of mercy for sinners, 1160

I promise those who venerate the Image ..., 48

I protect the proclaimers of mercy, 378

I receive worship by the Feast, 1048

I reign in a soul that loves, 1489

I reward your purity of intention, 1566

I see your love purer than the angels, 1061

I set a cherub to guard the gate, 1271

I shield souls who turn to me, 1682

I speak through the priest, 456

I suffer even more than you see, 445

I suffer ingratitude from chosen souls, 580

I teach you humility, 184

I thirst, 583

I thirst for the salvation of souls, 1032

I thirst for your love, 1542

I thought of you before you existed, 1292

I took away your ability to con-fess "faults," 1802

I unite Myself closer than others, 1546

I wait for souls, 1447

I waited to share suffering, 348

I want a novena of Chaplets for Poland, 714

I want her more obedient, 354

I want the Image to be publicly venerated, 341

I want the New Congregation to be modeled on His life, 438

I want this Image blessed on the Feast of Mercy, 49

I want to fill souls with love, 1017

I want to repose in your heart, 866

I want to rest in your heart, 339, 866

I want to see you as a sacrifice of living love, 1767

I want to teach you Myself, 1147

I want to teach you spiritual childhood, 1481

I want you to be My spouse, 912

I want you to write now, 1782

I was closer to you in dryness than in ecstasy, 1246

I will answer through your confessor, 290

I will answer you through your director, 145

I will be with you always, do not rely on creatures, 295

I will destroy convents and churches, 1702

I will direct your retreat, 1709, 1752

I will give a sign to Mother about the Image, 51

I will give you nothing beyond your strength, 1491

I will give you visible help [in

116

Father Sopocko], 53

I will leave this house, 44

I will let you know the time of death, 1539

I will make it [victim offering] known to you tomorrow, 135

I will not leave you in exile long, 1539

I will not leave you long in this community, 776

I will remove all doubts in this retreat, 169

I will reply through the mouth of the priest, 463

I will send you two sisters, 1494

I will speak through the retreat master, 1101

I will speak to you on this retreat through the priest, 456

I will strengthen you [lifting potato pot], 65

I will teach you, 1147

I would create a new world for you, 587

I yearn for souls, 206

If a soul does not exercise mercy somehow, it will not obtain mercy at judgment, 1317

If it hadn't been for this imperfection you would not have come to Me, 1293

If sinners bring all graces to nought, I leave them alone, 1728

If sinners knew My mercy, they would not perish, 1396

If souls would only turn to Me, 1683

If the priest had not brought Communion I would have come, 1459

If you leave this convent, 19

If you neglect the matter of painting the Image ..., 154

Image, 49, 51, 299, 354

Image a vessel of mercy, 327

Image, neglect of painting, 154

Imagine you are sovereign, 229

Immerse yourself in My mercy, 1361

Imperfections in chosen souls wound Me, 580

In Confession I am there hidden by the priest, 1602

In Confession the misery of the soul meets the God of Mercy, 1602

In feeling My suffering, you conform to Me, 1697

In heaven you will rejoice at your present suffering, 1786, 1787

In My Heart [the priest was], 442

In response to intercession, 1610

In the Host is your power, 616

In the Old Covenant I sent thunderbolts, today I send mercy, 1588

In this retreat I will keep you close to My Heart, 730

Indifference in Holy Communion, 1447

Ingratitude, 1537, 1538

Inscription, "Jesus, I trust in You," 327

Inscription of Image, 88

Instructs about the Novena to Divine Mercy, 1209

Interior life, 1685

Interior life of humility, 1701

It displeases Me that you did not ask for Father Andrasz, 1460

It pleases Me that you are writing faithfully, 1667

It will not be long, 865, 1787

It won't be long, 858

Join your sufferings to Mine for

infinite value, 1512

Judging others, 1528

Judgment of sinners, 1160

Judgment of the convent, 44

Judgment on convents and churches, 1702

Just a few more drops in your chalice, 694

Know My mercy, 730

Know that Satan hates you, 412

Know there is a great abyss between you and Me, filled by My mercy, 1572

Knowledge of self as misery, 718

Knowledge of souls given for conversion, 1357

Lack of awareness of My presence should not be an obatacle to your action, 1181

Lack of trust, 367

Language of the heart is pleasing, 797

Learn that no human entirely understands a soul, 1487

Leaving the convent, 19

Let sinners not fear to approach Me, even if sins are like the grains of sands, 1059

Let sinners trust in mercy, 1146

Let the rays of grace enter, 1486

Let those striving for perfection adore My mercy, 1578

Light of the moon and stars are like religious and faithful, 424

Listen to your Merciful Father, 1486

Listening in the heart, 584

Live according to My will, 443

Living in God's will, 443

Lock yourself in My Heart [in spiritual warfare], 1760

Look at My Merciful Heart, 177 (see also **Gaze**)

Look at Whom you married, 252

Look into My Heart and see mercy for sinners, 1663

Look into My Merciful Heart and reflect its compassion, 1688

Look into the abyss of My mercy, 206

Loss of souls, grieves, 1397

Love, 29

Love and humility, 512

Love and pray for those who cause suffering, 1628

Love brought Me here and keeps Me here, 576

Love dissipates difficulties, 1643

Love everyone: reflect My mercy, 1695

Love neighbor as the Eucharist, 285

Love of neighbor, 1768

Love those who cause you suffering, 1628

Lukewarm communicants, 1288

Make a novena before the Feast for Mercy to be known, 1059

Make a novena for Poland, 59

Make a novena of Chaplets, 796

Make a novena of Holy Hours with Mary, 32

Make reparation to My justice, 873

Mankind will have no peace until …, 300

Many souls are drawn by Image, 1379

May your heart be joyful, 415

Meditate on the Incarnation, 332

Meditate on John 15, 1757 (see also **Sacred Scripture**)

Meditate on John 19, 1765

Meditate on John 21, 1773

Meditate on Jonah, 331

Meditate on My Passion, 186, 332, 369, 1184, 1512, 1657

Meditation on the Church, 1758

Mercy, 206, 300, 301, 417 (see also **Mercy**)

Mercy, trust, 367 (see also **Trust**)

Mercy a shield at death, 1540

Mercy and distrust, 379

Mercy as a defense, 1516

Mercy before justice, 1588

Mercy for sinners, 367, 1146, 1396

Mercy from the wounded Heart, 1190

Mercy in suffering, 282

Mercy is drawn by one vessel: trust, 1578

Mercy is the sign for the end times, 848

Mercy the source of peace, 699

Mercy to sinners, 1665

Mercy to those in misery, 1182

Miracle of mercy [Confession] restores a soul, 1448

Miracles of mercy take place in Confession, 1448

Mirroring mercy, 1148

Misery does not hinder mercy, 1182

Misery does not stop Me, only pride, 1563

Mission of Sister Faustina: write about mercy, 1567

Mission of the New Congregation, 570

Model your life after My Merciful Heart, 167

Model your life on My Heart, 1701

More a soul trusts the more it receives, 1578

More glory given by obedience than prayers and mortifica-tions, 894

More value to meditate on Passion than scourging self, 369

Mortifying self-will lets Mine reign, 365

Most pleasing to Me is your preparation for Communion, 1824

My delight is to be united with you, 570

My eyes rest with pleasure upon this house, 280

My favor rests on you, 1774

My gaze from the Image ..., 326

My gaze is fixed on him [Father Sopocko], 86

My grace turns away from the proud to the humble, 1602

My Heart desires to be loved, 1703

My Heart drinks ingratitude of souls, 367

My Heart finds disappointment if there is not complete sur-render, 367

My Heart is fountain of mercy for the trusting, 1520

My Heart is full of love and mercy, 1447

My Heart is moved by mercy toward you, 282

My Heart overflows with mercy, 367

My Heart rejoices at purity of intention and humiliation, 1566

My Heart rejoices in the title of Mercy, 300

My Heart rejoices when a sinner returns, 1728

My host, you are My refresh-ment, 1056

My joy, 27

My law is founded on love, 1478

My life from birth to cross will be your rule, 526

My love burns for souls, 186

My mercy does not want this [purgatory], 20

My mercy fills the great abyss, 1576

My mercy is a sign for the end times, 848

My mercy is confirmed in My every work, 723

My mercy is greater than any can imagine, 699

My mercy knows no bounds, 718

My mercy passes into souls through My Heart as a crystal, 528

My mercy pursues sinners, 1728

My Secretary, write about My mercy toward sinners, 1275

My Secretary, write that I am the spiritual guide of souls, 1784

My Spirit rests on you, 346

My will is not yet fulfilled, you will suffer, 675

Never trust in yourself, 1760

Never withdraw your efforts, 1374

New Congregation pleading for mercy, 531

New Congregation, 463

New Congregation is My doing, 586

No escaping mercy, 1728

Not all receive Communion with living faith, 1407

Not feeling suffering does not mean a soul in grace, 1357

Not in the beauty of the color ... but in grace, 313

Nothing can oppose My will, 1531

Novena before the Feast, 1209

Now your smallest acts are a delight to Me [aftervictim oblation], 137

Obedience, 381, 535 (see also **Obedience**)

Obedience and love is better than mortification, 1023

Obedience and mortification, 365

Obedience is more pleasing than penance, 1023

Obedience is more valuable than penances, 933

Obedience to her confessor, 639, 933

Of yourself you are nothing, 1559

Offer expiation, 39

Offer me your misery, 1318, 1775

Offer of creating a new world, 587

Offer your Masses in expiation for a city, 39

Offering of self, 308, 309

On blessings and gratitude, 719

On income for the New Congregation: trust, 548

On mercy and trust, 718

On the Feast bring fainting souls to mercy, 206

On the Feast the floodgates are open, 699

On weakness, 722

One price for souls; suffering with Christ, 324

Only by grace you share in eternal life, 1559

Only love satisfies, 1023

Only mortal sin drives Me out, 1181

Open your heart only to your

confessor, 1163

Openness to confessor, 269

Our hearts are joined forever [final vows], 238

Overcoming difficulties by love, 1643

Pain if you leave, 19

Pain in your heart brought solace to My Heart, 445

Pained by spurned love more than a mother, 1447

Paint an Image, 47 (see also **Image**)

Patience, 1587 (see also **Virtues**)

Patience, it won't be long, 858

Pay attention to the grace, not the vessel, 1599

Peace be with you, 1067, 1069

Peace, I am arranging things with the superiors, 215

Peace, you have a share in My Passion, now in My joy, 205

Peace, you will understand everything through Father Andrasz, 219

Penetrate into the spirit of My poverty, 532

Penetrate My Spirit of meekness and humility, 526

Perfection, 1165

Persecution because of work of mercy is in store, 966

Persevere in prayer, 157

Pity, 286

Plead for mercy as a Congregation, 435 (see also **Intercession**)

Pleased by suffering, 279

Pleased with home visit, 404

Pleased with the ardor of the heart, 826

Pleased with trust, 324

Pleasure in this house, 280

Points of meditation, 149

Poverty of the New Congregation, 532

Power of sacrifice lies in the will, 1767

Power of sacrifice with love, 1316-1317

Practice humility, purity and love, 1779 (see also **Mary, Mother of God: Words of Our Lady**)

Pray Chaplet without ceasing, 687

Pray for priests, 980

Pray for Russia, 818

Pray for sinners, 1397

Pray for souls not to fear confession, 975

Pray for student, 288, 1603

Pray much for the dying, 1777

Pray: O Blood and Water ..., 187, 309

Prayer intention for the convent accepted for others, 1714

Prayer [of presence] is pleasing to, 691

Prayer most pleasing for sinners, 1397

Prepare for My final coming, 429

Prepare for suffering, 488

Preparing for His coming, 429 (see also **Second Coming**)

Presence of Jesus, 1181

Presence of Jesus in dryness, 1246

Present all My demands clearly to confessor, 1644

Priest acts in My place, 331

Priest is speaking particularly to you, 381

Priest was in My Heart, 442

Priests are to tell all about mercy on the Feast, 570

Priests will recommend the

Chaplet, 687

Proclaim My mercy, 1142

Proclaim that mercy is the greatest attribute, 301

Proclaiming mercy, 341, 378, 1519

Promises about the Chaplet, 811

Protection at the gate, 1271

Purgatory, 20, 36

Pure soul is humble, 576

Purpose of your companions is to reconcile earth with heaven, 531

Put his [confessor's] judgment above My demands, 895

Rays denote Blood and Water, 299

Rays of mercy will pass through you to the world, 441

Read chapter 15 of Saint John's Gospel, 1757 (see also **Sacred Scripture**)

Read chapter 19 of Saint John's Gospel, 1765

Read chapter 21 of Saint John's Gospel, 1773

Rebuke for not asking for a confessor, 1460

Reflect on My words, 584

Regarding a person, his heart is a heaven, 574

Rely on your confessor even in smallest things, 639

Remain as a child, 295

Remain faithful to My grace, 1166

Resolution to be a saint pleases Me, 1361 (see also 1333, 1361, 1362, 1372)

Respond to Father Andrasz's concern about sudden apparitions, 1069

Responding to temptation, 1560

Rest my child, 1011

Rest on My Heart, 902, 945

Rest on My Shoulder, 498

Resting in her hands, 160

Retreat will be an uninterrupted contemplation, 1327

Return of a sinner gives Me greatest praise, 378

Return to your room and write, 1782

Rule of the New Congregation, 526

Sacred Heart with rays, 177 (see also **Merciful Heart of Jesus**)

Sacrifice and love by souls sustains the world, 367

Sacrifice and prayer, 1767

Sad over distrust and ingratitude, 580, 581

Saddened by souls who do not love, 1478

Satan gained nothing by tempting, 1499

Satan is trying to disturb your peace, 1802

Say the Chaplet, 810

Say the Chaplet and obtain what you ask, 1731

Say the Chaplet for a dying sinner, 811, 1565, 1797

Say the Chaplet unceasingly, 687

See how little you have written about My mercy for sinners, 1665b

See My mercy for sinners, 1665a

See what love of souls has done to Me, 268

Seek strength in My Passion, 654

Seldom souls unite with Me in Communion, 1447

Set little store on what people say, 1685

Share in redemption, 310

Sharing in His Passion, 445,

446, 1053, 1054

Signature of Image, 88, 327

Silence, 1164

Silence, need for, 1008, 1717

Simplicity, 335

Simplicity more pleasing than mortifications, 1617

Simplicity of love from the heart, 797

Sinners will repent at the words of priests on mercy, 1521

Sisters are to pray the Chaplet, 714

Sooner heaven and earth will pass than My mercy not embrace a trusting soul, 1777

Sorrow over not receiving Communion, 612

Soul steeped in darkness, confide in God, 1486

Soul that doesn't know self can't judge others, 1528

Soul that trusts will radiate mercy, 1074

Soul who has complete trust is Most dear, 453

Souls are sanctified by trust, 1578

Souls converted by prayer, 640

Souls like Me in suffering will be like Me in glory, 446

Souls perish in spite of My Passion, 965

Souls should reflect My mercy, 1148

Souls strengthened by the Image, 1379

Souls that appeal to My mercy delight Me, 1146

Souls that proclaim My mercy I deal with mercy at death, 379

Souls that trust radiate to others, 1074

Souls will be sanctified by

works of mercy, 966

Spark from Poland, 1732

Speak freely to Mother Superior [Irene] about mercy, 1519

Speak to sinners of My mercy, 1396

Speak to world about My mercy, 848

Speaks with various souls, 1485-1489

Special union with Sister Faustina, 587

Spiritual director's words are His, 1308

Spiritual life: abide in Me continually; entrust self to Me, 1685

Spiritual mercy is always possible, 1317

Spiritual warfare, 1760

Spread the honor of My mercy, 1075

Stand ready, I will come unexpectedly, 854

Stay home, 64

Story of love, 229

Strength from My Passion, 654

Strengthen yourself for combat, 145

Students, 288

Submission to His will, 904, 954

Suffering, 289, 694

Suffering for a while, 154

Suffering for souls, 67

Suffering is a grace, 1697

Suffering is a sign of My presence, 669

Suffering needed for souls, 1612

Suffering of Jesus in some communicants, 1598

Suffering of the pure of soul, 324

Suffering until death, 1597

Suffering will be a sign I am with you, 669

Suffering will end soon, 152

Super abundance of grace to the humble, 1293

[Superior's will] is My will, 329

Take as many graces as you can carry, that others spurn, 454

Take this ciborium to the tabernacle; treat sisters the same, 285

Take the vessel of trust and draw mercy, 1488

Taking her heart, 42

Talk to Me in simplicity, 921

Talk to the men at the gate as you talk to Me, 1377

Task of this life and the next, exhort souls to trust, 1452 (see also **Mission**)

Teaches sister Faustina to suffer, 1626

Tell aching humanity to snuggle close, 1074

Tell all the sisters ..., 353

Tell everything to your confessor, 232

Tell him [Father Sopocko] not to fear, 90

Tell Me about everything, 921

Tell Me your desires, 1489

Tell Mother about sins in the house, 45

Tell Mother I took your heart, 42

Tell Mother two sisters are in danger of sin, 43

Tell Mother what displeases Me, 191

Tell Mother you are a most faithful daughter of the order, 1130

Tell Mother you are in good health, 1091

Tell people I am Mercy Itself, 1074

Tell priests about My mercy, 177

Tell sinners I wait for them, 1728

Tell sinners no one will escape My hands, 1728

Tell souls not to place obstacles to My mercy, 1577

Tell souls they draw grace by trust, 1602

Tell souls to look for solace in the tribunal of mercy, 148

Tell the confessor that this is My work, 645

Tell the friend of My Heart I use feeble creatures, 498

Tell the priest, 12

Tell the priest to preach on mercy on the Feast, 1072

Tell the superior you are in good health, 1091

Tell the world about My mercy, 164, 699, 848, 1074

Tell your confessor everything, 645

Tell your confessor that I commune in an intimate way, 1069

Thank you for sharing My sufferings, 1061

Thanksgiving opens up treasures of graces, 1489

There will be darkness and a sign of the cross in the sky, 83

There will be peace at death for the trusting, 1520

These are Hosts of those converted, 640

These Hosts [full ciboriurm] received by souls converted by your prayers and suffering, 709

This is how you are to be

clothed, 526

This is My faithful servant [Father Sopocko], 263

This prayer will appease My wrath, "Eternal Father ...," 476

This soul is dear to me, 1671

Those who say the Chaplet will be embraced by mercy, 754

Though God, I cannot help a soul that scorns Me, having a free will, 580

Though you may not feel My presence [in suffering], I am always with you, 1767

Three o'clock hour, 1572

Through his [Father Sopocko] work more souls will come to mercy than by absolving, 1256

Through misery I show My power of mercy, 133

Through the Chaplet you will obtain everything, 1731

To Mother Superior, 191

To priests, 50, 177, 570, 687, 1521

To suffering soul, do not lose heart, 1487

To suffering soul, no way to heaven except the cross, 1487

To suffering soul, talk simply to Me 1487

To suffering soul, what hinders you? 1487

To the Superior, 28, 32, 45

To whom are you taking these flowers? 71

Today bring to Me all devout, 1214

Today bring to Me all mankind, 1210

Today bring to Me priests and religious, 1212

Today bring to Me the luke-warm, 1228

Today bring to Me the meek, 1220

Today bring to Me the pagans, 1216

Today bring to Me the souls in purgatory, 1226

Today bring to Me the souls of heretics, 1216

Today bring to Me those who venerate My mercy, 1224

Transgressions against your confessor touch Me, 145

Tribunal of mercy, 975, 1448

True greatness is in loving God in humility, 424, 427

Trust in My mercy in the midst of suffering, 1452

Underline the Lord's words, advice of Father Andrasz, 967

Union, 1700

Union with Jesus, 1754

Unite yourself with Me, 1543, 1544

Unpleasant to be received by a resisting soul, 1658

Until Easter you will feel My presence, 413

Use the graces others spurn, 454

Value of love, 576

Veneration of the Image, 414

Voluntary offenses obstruct grace, 1641

Weakness, 722

What are you afraid of, 527

What are you thinking, 960

What do you desire to tell Me? [regarding escape from hell], 873

What graces I grant to those who say the Chaplet, 848

What you have written is but a drop in the ocean, 1273

What you have written is Mine, 1667

What you said is true; you are very miserable, 881

Whatever you do to others, you do to Me, 1029

When a soul repents there is no limit to My mercy, 1728

When you go to Confession, My Blood and Water flow down, 1602

Where are you going? 673

While there is time come to My mercy, 848

Who knows about this Feast? 341

Why are you fearful; trust Me, 453, 527, 922

Why are you weeping, 596

Why fear to do My will, 489

Why He came as a beggar boy, 1312, 1313

Will of God, 372

Win souls and encourage trust, 1690

With a despairing soul, 1486

With no other soul do I unite Myself as closely, 587

With sinful soul, 1485

With suffering soul, 1487

Words of the confessor are Mine, 967, 968

Work of mercy is Mine, 1667

World hates and persecutes you, 1487

Worship My mercy, 998

Wound in My Heart is source of all mercy, 1190

Write about mercy and trust, 1567 (see also **Write/Writing**)

Write and proclaim My mercy but also beg mercy for sinners, 1160

Write every sentence I tell you about My mercy, 1142

Write everything about goodness, 459, 1605

Write everything about My mercy, 1605, 1693 (see also **Work of Mercy**)

Write for souls, 895

Write, I delight to come to hearts, 1683

Write, I speak to sinners in many ways, 1728

Write in all your free time, 1567

Write more on mercy, 1273

Write of My mercy, 1448

Write, tell souls of My mercy, 965

Write that I want to pour out My mercy, 1784

Write, those who glorify mercy will be shielded, 1540

You are a disciple of a crucified Master, 1513

You are a living host, 1826

You are a sweet grape in a chosen cluster, 393

You are a witness of My mercy, 417

You are administrator of My mercy, 570

You are already tasting what others will in eternity, 969

You are close to My Heart because you are a child, 1617

You are dispenser of My mercy, 580

You are guilty of one day in purgatory, 36

You are in My Heart, 1133

You are incapable of receiving graces without help, 738

You are living for souls, 67

You are more pleasing than the angelic chorus, 1489

You are most faithful, 1130

You are My delight; for your sake I bless the earth, 431

You are My delightful dwelling, 346

You are My great joy, your love and humility make Me leave heaven, 512

You are My Heart, 1666

You are My joy [first vows], 27

You are My well-beloved daughter, 1681

You are our dwelling place, 451

You are refreshment in torment, 1056, 1058

You are solace in My dying hour, 310

You are solace in torments, 1058

You are the delight of My Heart, 1176, 1193, 1489

You are the saint of the congregation, 1333, 1360, 1361, 1410, 1571, 1650

You are the secretary of My mercy, 1605

You are to be My living reflection, 1446

You are to defend them [children] from evil, 765

You are united with me in life and death, 1552

You ask too much, 961

You can do nothing by yourself, 429

You caused Me sorrow by not uniting in Holy Communion, 612

Your efforts are pleasing, 757

You give Me greatest glory by fulfilling My desires, 500

You give Me greatest glory in submitting to My will, 954

You glorify Me by submitting to My will, 904

You have experienced in three

hours the night of suffering, 1054

You have great rights over My Heart, 718

You have permission to begin the three day retreat, 1752

You haven't written everything about My goodness, 459

You know well the depths of My mercy, 873, 1777

You make Me happy by telling the world of My mercy, 164

You must be destroyed in the secret depths, 1767

You please Me by your humility, 1563

You please Me most by your suffering, 279

You please Me most meditating on My Passion, 1512

You rely too much on self, 1488

You see My hands, 1722

You shall experience My goodness, 1707

You still must suffer, fear not, 675

You tie My hands and disarm My anger, 1722

You were counting too much on yourself, 1087

You will be imbued with My mercy, 167

You will find rest only on My Heart, 36

You will not be in good health, 1464

You will rejoice in heaven over these days of suffering, 1787

You will save more souls by prayer and suffering than a missionary by sermons, 1767 (see also**Mission**)

You will suffer on earth, 36

Your chastity should be greater

than the angels, 534

Your compassion refreshes Me, 1657, 1664

Your confidence restrains My justice, 198

Your demands are too great, but I comply, 961

Your every stirring is reflected in My Heart, 1700

Your heart is a dwelling, 723

Your heart is My heaven, 238

Your heart is My repose, 339

Your heart is to be an abiding place of My mercy, 1777

Your hour has not yet come, you will bear witness to My mercy, 689

Your humility draws Me down from My throne, 1109

Your love binds My hands, 1193

Your love compensates for coldness of many, 1816

Your love is a consolation to Me in the garden, 1664

Your love restrains My justice, 198

Your misery is consumed in mercy by humility, 178

Your mission is to win souls by prayer and suffering and to encourage trust, 1690 (see also **Mission**)

Your prayer is pleasing, 691

Your prayers are accepted for others' intentions, 1714

Your preparation for Communion pleases Me, 1824

Your sacrifice must be silent, hidden, loving, pure, humble, 1767

Your soul is filled with My love, 1643

Your spiritual director and I are one, 1308

Your spiritual director replaces Me like a veil, 1308

Your struggle will end with death, 1597

Your suffering brought mercy to many, 1459

Your sufferings obtain mercy for many, 1458, 1459

Your trust forces Me to grant graces, 718

Your writing bears the seal of obedience, 1567

Yours is an exclusive intimacy with Me, 1693

Work of Mercy (Spread of the Devotion)

(see also **Chaplet, Deeds of Mercy, Feast, Hour of Great Mercy, Image, Intercession, Mercy, Novena, Oblation**)

Account of, on judgment day, 660

All depends on God's will, 1642

Apparent destruction, 378, 1389

Article on mercy, 1081, 1082

Blessing on one spreading the devotion, 1083

Booklet of Chaplet, Litany and Novena, 1379

Bound to, 638

Deep knowledge, 1143

Deep peace about the future of the work, 1659

Desire to act, 1027

Despite misery, do what you can, 881

Despite problems with the Image, the mercy of God will triumph, 1789

Difficulties overcome by God's love, 1643

Disputes over the Feast, 1110

Do all obedience allows, 1644

Do what can be done, 1295

Drawn by a mysterious force, 1027

Effect of Father Sopocko's work, 1390

Effect on souls, 1379

Father Andrasz advises prayer for, 1618

Father Sopocko and, 421, 1608

Father Sopocko on the Feast, Novena, Chaplet and Image, 1254, 1255

Faustina and, 154, 281, 1401, 1530, 1643, 1644

Future results of, 1300

Gives glory to God, 859

Glorifying God, 1463

God's love for those who spread mercy, 962

God's work, 764, 1595, 1667

Greater the work, the greater the storms, 1401, 1402

Heroic efforts, 838

Hinderance to, 1295

Image and cards being printed, 1299

In difficulties God is working, 764

In God's will, 1642

Is God's work, 711

Jesus asks to write about external matters, 1457

Likened to the Eucharist, 285

Linked with work of Redemption, 89

Meets with opposition, 270

Mission of Sister Faustina to make known God's mercy and encourage trust, 1567 (see also **Mission**)

Mother Superior's role, 1296 (see also **Mother Superior General**)

Need patience, 270

Never withdraw your efforts, 1374

New health and strength for, 1090

Not overcome by enemies' attack, 1659

Nothing can oppose it, 1531

Obedience, 523 (see also **Obedience**)

Oblation for, 1680 (see also **Oblation**)

Office and task of her whole life, 1567 (see also **Mission**)

Opposed by Satan, 812, 1115 (see also **Spiritual Warfare**)

Opposition to, 1272

Pleasing to God, 962

Prayer to hasten the Feast, 1530, 1531

Problems of writing diary, 839 (see also **Write/Writing**)

Prohibition, 378, 1389

Role of Mother superior [Irene], 1296, 1301 (see also **Mother Superior/ General**)

Salvation for many, 1300

Satan's anger at, 1583 (see also **Spiritual Warfare**)

Source of suffering, 786

Spiritual director orders to write, 6 (see also **Write/Writing**)

Spread by a soul, 1083

Spread by Father Sopocko, 1256

Spread the devotion, 1074, 1075

Suffering of Father Sopocko, 1390

Suffering of priest, 838 (see also **Father Sopocko**)

Suffering of priest from opposition, 1272

Support by Mother Irene, 1301

Tensions about the Feast, 1463

The trials of the work, 1608

Three aspects, 1155

Threefold; deed, word, prayer, 1158

Time of apparent destruction, 378, 1389

Time of destruction, 1659

To be done despite weakness, 787

Under trial, 1610

Undergoing trials, 1608

Underlining words of Jesus in diary, 959

Urge to act, 1389

Valued by intention, 822

Vision of examination of writing, 1045

Ways to take part in, 1155-1158

Words of Jesus, (see also **Words of Jesus**)

    all this work and writing is Mine, 1667 (see also **Write/Writing**)

    being a pliant tool, 1359

    continue in your efforts, 1374

    devote all your free time to writing, 1567, 1693 (see also **Write/Writing**)

    do all you can, 1644

    do all you can for this work, 998, 1074

    do not be discouraged with difficulties, 1142

    fall of angels, 1331

    Father Sopocko's work at the desk, 1256

    hinderance to the work of mercy, 1295

    how little you have written about mercy, 1665, 1666

    I will protect those who spread the veneration of My mercy, 1075

    proclaiming mercy, 1519

    response to difficulties, 1295

    write down everything for souls, 1142

    write everything about My goodness, 459 (see also **Write/Writing**)

    write everything about My mercy, 1605, 1693

    write for souls, 895

    write now, 1782

    writing more on mercy, 1273

Words written are inadequate to describe God's mercy, 1659

Works of Father Sopocko, 1401

Works of Jesus, 895, 1667

Writing for others, 1471, 1635

Writing under obedience, 1006

Write/Writing
(see also **Work of Mercy**)

About external matters as well as graces, 1457

About goodness of God, 1605

About mercy for souls, 1146

About mercy, Satan's attack, 713 (see also **Spiritual Warfare**)

All written for sick souls who suffer neglect, 1635

All your free time, 1567

And beg for mercy, 1160

Because of obedience, 523 (see also **Obedience**)

Commanded, 1006

Difficulty in, 839

Everything about mercy, 1693

Examined by priests, 1045

Fathers Sopocko and Andrasz, like lightening, 675

For souls, 895, 1142, 1317, 1471

God is Mercy Itself to the contrite, 1739

God's mercy pursues sinners, 1728

Goodness of God beyond writ-

ing, 1800

I am the spiritual guide of souls, 1784

Importance of Father Sopocko's, 1256

Is the way Jesus wishes, 1471

More on mercy, 1273

Not a single word was mine, 1667

Of glory of God's mercy, 1659

Of goodness and mercy of God, 1567

Of My mercy, 1448

Only a drop, 1666

Prayer to Holy Spirit, 1567

Satan warning against, 1138 (see also **Spiritual Warfare**)

So little written about mercy for sinners, 1665

Those who glorify mercy will be shielded, 1540

To distressed souls to trust, 1541

What comes to mind, 1605

Words are inadequate, 758

Under obedience, 523, 1568

Under obedience to Jesus and confessor, 895

Underlining of the Lord's words, 959, 967

Write now, 1782

9 781596 141377